DATE		

a week in winter

barth landor

a week in winter

barth landor

the permanent press
sag harbor, new york 11963

Copyright© 2004 by Barth Landor

Library of Congress Cataloging-in-Publication Data

Landor, Barth.
   A week in winter : a novel / by Barth Landor.
      p. cm.
   ISBN 1-57962-099-X (alk. paper)
   1. Americans—Europe, Eastern—Fiction. 2. Refugees,
   Jewish—Fiction. 3. Europe, Eastern—Fiction. 4. Jewish
   families—Fiction. 5. Antisemitism—Fiction. 6.
   Ambassadors—Fiction. 7. Diplomats—Fiction. I. Title.

   PS3612.A5485W44 2004
   813'.6—dc22

                                        2003066032

Printed in The United States of America

THE PERMANENT PRESS
4170 Noyac Road
Sag Harbor, NY 11963

To my parents - my mother and the memory
of my father - I dedicate this book

PART ONE

MONDAY

Evening

-Will you tell me a story?

-Not tonight. It's late.

-Just a short one. Please?

-I'll sing a song instead.

-No—a story.

-Then I'll sing a story.

-How can you sing a story?

-"Ramblin Boy" is a story, and it's also a song.

-No it's not. It's just a song.

-Well, some people sing their stories. Hop on down and flush.

-Wait, Daddy. I've got a great idea. First you can tell a really short story -

-Flush. Teethbrush.

-I want to brush my own teeth.

-No. Open up.

-Mommy says I can when I'm six.

-When you're six.

-Daddy?

-Don't talk. Now spit out. OK, Jack, get into bed.

-Daddy?

-What.

-Do grownups' teeth ever fall out?

-They do sometimes.

-Do new ones grow back?

-No. Grownups have to go to the dentist for new teeth.

11

-Are they real?

-You mean the dentists?

-No, the teeth.

-No. But sometimes they're made of gold.

-They are really?

-Sure. And silver, too.

-Wouldn't it be funny if I grew a gold tooth?

-You will if you get to bed on time.

-No, I won't.

-Come on, under the sheets we go. I'll tell you a very short story.

-Tell one about kindergarten.

-Only if you're quiet.

-About a boy in kindergarten.

-Shh ... Shh ... We'll have lots of talking tomorrow ... now it's listening time ... Put your head on the pillow ... Once there was a boy ...

One arrives at this hour hardly able to go on. Here it is only Jack's bedtime, and already I'm sinking under the accumulations of a day: the working, commuting, caretaking, what one heard and said and saw, and wished one hadn't, and then too much wine at dinner. I've spent my energy hauling around the day's rags and bones, so that now, with an evening before me to provide some peace and solitude, I have just enough strength to go flop on my bed and utter a short prayer for the revival of my spirit tomorrow. It's only now, when all the activity of the day is finally behind me, that I realize the full cost of my exertions, like that Greek runner setting off eagerly from Marathon with his news of victory in war, dreaming as he ran of a bath and a meal and the joy of regaling his countrymen with tales of triumph, who reached Athens after all those miles only to drop down dead. Here I am at last at Athens—I've gotten food into Jack and Jack into bed—and now I think I'll give up.

-Daddy?
-What, honey?
-Will you come lie next to me?
-No, Jack, we've had our story and now it's sleeptime. I'll give you a kiss, though.
-Will you come back to check on me?
-I will if you go to sleep.

Directly to bed, then—there's nothing else I could do, not even stop to undress. I'm too weak to occupy myself any longer in this day. I want only to be released from it, delivered into the hours of forgetting, those sweet hours of succumbing, left to lie here in my crumpled clothing until morning comes. Tonight it's either oblivion or pottering about, which is all I could hope for, and I choose sleep. I won't stir unless Jack cries out.

That long-distance messenger at Marathon, dimmed almost into darkness by the millennia: he really did live. You could have talked with him about the weather or asked him about his running. He was human like us, until that day he became far more human. The last three or four miles of that lonely run must have tortured him, his body racked with pain, unlike any he would ever have known. Perhaps he was desperate to stop and rest, but thought that every minute spent in not getting closer to Athens meant a minute of disloyalty to Greece. My own weariness has precious little in common with his; on the contrary, far from having exhausted my strength on some higher

13

purpose, I have only shuffled my way from dawn to dusk, through the office talk and office tensions, work, and the conversations about work. Heroism has not figured into my waking hours. I have had to endure nothing worse than the spectacle, a displeasing one to be sure, of my colleagues working themselves into various states of anxiety over the announcement that we would be honored this very Friday by a visit from the ambassador. It would have been much easier to announce that on Friday the world would turn to ice. Was it really true: Ambassador Todd, that prominent personage, distant head of our hierarchy, was actually making a trip in a few short days to our remote site, this little satellite of the Embassy? I couldn't help but appreciate the comic possibilities here, starting with the old case of mistaken identity: the first person to arrive at the gates of our consulate on Friday is not the ambassador himself but some vagabond whom we confuse for the esteemed guest, etc. It's a situation begging for farce.

But I'd say there was a total lack of mirth at that meeting. No scenarios of merry mix-ups could have stood in the way of that stampede of questions: What was he coming for? Had something happened? Were we being subjected to a review? Why had we been given such short notice?—none of which was answered with any assurance. I wish I'd posed a few questions of my own: Would we be quite sure that the chap who arrived was actually Ambassador Todd, and would it not be prudent to ask him to bring along some identification, a driver's license or a set of fingerprints? And perhaps we should also check for distinguishing marks on his person, which was not to say that he had to submit to a physical exam, one just didn't want to be deceived by some impostor.

However, I did not add my own voice to the clamor, and I suppose I appeared inadequately affected. I had only a moment of uneasiness, and not over the news itself; when Fitch informed us all of the ambassador's visit—and quite brusquely, too, not in the manner of one who wishes to inform, but rather to warn—he had been staring straight at me. It was an improbable scene: Fitch facing us at the conference table along which all ten or eleven of us were ranged, gripping a sheaf of papers while he delivered almost all of his little speech with his gaze fixed squarely upon mine. But this visit can have nothing to do with me personally. I'm not acquainted with the ambassador at all, I'm pretty sure I haven't bungled some administrative matter requiring the fellow to come sort it all out, and I certainly don't merit any special commendation from him. And it's clear that Fitch is also in the dark about the reason for the visit. Despite the bluster in his tone and the rather violent way he waved about those papers, all of his responses were just variations on the theme of not having a damn clue, a virtuoso performance elaborating richly on the phrase 'I don't know'.

What could have been the meaning of that look of his? Even though there seems to be ill will between us, in the circumstances it makes no sense to me. Maybe I only imagined it. No one else seemed to notice; at least no one said anything to me when the meeting broke up, nor did he himself address me afterwards. I could more easily shrug off the episode if there wasn't a history here, but I can't say if it's a history of Fitch's disdain for me or just of my suspecting it.

My mind tonight is a crowded cattle-car, thoughts herded in pell-mell, pushed against each other, restless, making a commotion. I can't sleep, and yet I'm too weary to move. I feel as I do when I'm down with a fever: images jostle energetically, but my own strength is missing, my *anima*, the agent which puts motion in my limbs. If I could I would reach for a book, or put on some music, or light a cigar and ponder things, but my wherewithal's not there, and I don't know what's happened to it. It's not possibly on account of that silly meeting today that all the air's gone out of me—why, that was nothing more than passing half an hour. Afterwards I gave the matter no more attention, but went back to my desk and busied myself with paperwork, leaving others to hash over the news. I could, however, hear some of my colleagues from my cubicle, their talk loud and verbose, and whether or not this event was truly important to them I couldn't say, but it did definitely give them a topic to warm themselves with. My only comment on the subject all afternoon was made to Fitch, whose customary bustle seemed to have suddenly acquired a *raison d'être*. Seeing him in the corridor, I offered lamely, "That's quite an event we've got", and I regret having said even that, the way it so overstated my feelings. I believe that innocuous little remark of mine has chafed at me more than anything today; but is one instead to keep one's dignity intact by maintaining a contemptuous silence? It seems a waste of perfectly good silence.

O, work—by the end of the day it has intoxicated me, stupefied me. I come home with large traces of it in my blood and go to bed with it still in my system, and when I wake in the morning finally sober, I get up and go quaff some more. I suppose the whole business of that announcement today, Fitch frowning at me followed by the loud and lengthy colloquies of my rumormongering colleagues, really has acted on me like an extra glass or two. I've gone through my working hours reacting reasonably to things, having had no idea that there was another process underway, sapping me.

Perhaps, though, while I've been lying here groggily, some of my strength has returned; not much, but maybe I have something in me after all, enough for a small effort—the cigar might just be manageable. Now there would be a feat of sorts. This day thinks it's got me beat, but if I can get myself upright, I'll show it that I've got some puff in me. It would make being alive today worthwhile to blow smoke rings around this world-weariness. These moments of my own, so often stolen in the absence of daylight, early in the morning over coffee even before Jack is up, or late in the evening as my cares recede from me, recall me to the fragile possession of a self. To the cigar, then— may my thoughts set me free!

*

If Ellen were home tonight, I would try to keep the living room from filling up with smoke, opening windows or going into the kitchen. She doesn't favor the smell of cigars, unlike me—I luxuriate in this pungent haze, this air-thickening fug, the acrid odor of which seems to wrap around me like a cocoon. It's one of the few pleasures that I would really be sorry to give up, one that I would include on a list of the good things in life, sheepishly, at least, slipping it somewhere in the middle. I enjoy a kind of kinship with our cigar-smoking mailman, whose fumes are sometimes lingering in the lobby when I arrive home from work, and although he and I have never actually met, I feel that his smoke in our building connects us, especially because a good cigar is almost impossible to come by in this impoverished country which provides for its ordinary citizens only the barest and blandest of necessities. He must go to some effort to acquire them. I might have asked Ellen to pick up a box while she's in the States, some for him and some for me, but she wouldn't have had much enthusiasm for bringing back these malodorous objects. I'm happy to procure the tobacco leaf through channels at the consulate, as she does quite enough for me on these trips to America in replenishing our larder with strong things to drink—upon her return she unpacks bottles of whiskey and bags of coffee, which embarrasses me, since the point of these trips is hardly a hedonistic one, visiting her sick mother, but she knows without my having to speak of it that I do relish these scarcities.

In the lunch room recently I commented to my companions that what I missed most about America were the delights of the palate, most of all the imported foods that you could get in certain shops and neighborhoods in my native Chicago—I was thinking of kalamata olives and stuffed grape leaves, Russian dumplings, kosher pastries. A couple of my colleagues considered my remark rather frivolous; after all, we were living in a country whose inhabitants lacked much larger goods—democracy, freedom of speech, to say nothing of lesser luxuries like fruit and vegetables. Was it only finer foods that I felt nostalgic for? I tried to suggest that one could hardly use one's liberty better than to esteem things that were excellent; indeed, true gratitude for the richness of one's table seemed to me like a good way to be free. However, my meaning got distorted in the expressing of it. I said, "Frankly, I think more about a French cheese I once had called St. Nectaire than I do about democracy," an utterance which did not convey my thought at all, for my colleagues assumed that I was expounding some epicurean philosophy at the expense of our Founding Fathers, and Andrew Priestley looked at me as if I were a very foolish creature before abruptly dismissing me from his field of vision. But I had really been talking about the appreciation of particular things, and I should instead have given a more homely example, like that of the holy simpleton who arrives in heaven and can ask for anything he wants—eternal happiness, release from pain and suffering—but whose only request is to receive every morning a hot roll and coffee. In like manner I would understand it if my mailman ever went to America and spent his first day of newfound freedom searching for a cigar store.

I'm fairly sure that my lunchtime remark made its way to Fitch's ears, presumably via the indignant Priestley. Indeed, that afternoon I caught a glimpse of the two of them conversing earnestly in Fitch's office, and for days afterwards I sensed that Fitch was upset with me, but what solid proof did I have of it? If he seemed impatient when we discussed consular matters, even faintly hostile, or if he didn't bother to acknowledge me when we passed each other, there was nothing blatant in his anger, and I couldn't even be certain that Priestley had filled him in on the details of *le scandale du fromage*. I could accuse Fitch of nothing worse than a roughness in manner toward me, not worth thinking about; and yet I often find myself puzzling for half a day over some flash of his annoyance. It's this absurd worry about the opinion one's boss has of one which affects me—Fitch might as well be my sweetheart the way I mull over his gestures and non-gestures. And just like a lover he's distracted me tonight from my cigar, for instead of enjoying it as I intended, I've let my thoughts float workward.

But there's time left in this day to turn; time to stop the drift of my mind's flotsam; there's time yet to focus, focus. It would be an act of salvaging wreckage to collect and direct myself before bed—with a book, perhaps; it would be the achievement of my day, an entirely private one, it's true, but are the only valid deeds the witnessed ones? I like to think the opposite: the great enterprises take place within oneself. To my book, then—may the reading of it restore me to myself.

*

What would I do without these old authors? Who would I turn to if not to them—this smattering of men and women dotted across the millennia, speaking a language that speaks to me. These old books, with their outmoded words and customs and gods—they make a great show of belonging to a vanished time and place, whose ways have nothing in common with ours; but when you draw close the strange spectacle might just fade, and in its place stand a dear companion, and a teacher, too. Here I am reading about a subject whose every term should shoo me away—the intricacies of seventeenth-century Jesuit doctrine—a subject which at this late hour ought to be bringing sleep a lot closer. I would never presume to disturb the settled dust that these tenets have become over hundreds of years, but how I love to watch the way that Pascal disturbed them, and he did it back when such doctrines still had power to do harm. He wrote these *lettres provinciales* at great risk to himself, daring to suggest that if one Jesuit condemns, say, murder, and another Jesuit justifies the same kind of murder, and they both rely on Jesuit doctrine to make their case, then there is actually a contradiction here. For pointing this out, he had the police on his trail, and a French parliament banning his letters, because the gravest crime of all was not, say, murder, but rather, disagreeing with the Jesuits. As long as you remained within the order, no outlandish notion was denied you. How silly these self-inflating Pooh-Bahs seem today, all their elaborate and multitudinous treatises come to nothing, whereas Pascal: his voice reaches me across the nations and generations; he wakes me up.

He woke me up this morning, too, as I read this volume on the train, his words like a patch of vivid color on a background of gray—and then with a sigh I arrived at the office and tossed the book on my desk, my now-sharpened wits about to undergo the daily dulling. I prepared myself for the day's tasks; but the book lying there on the desk, exposed, as it were, made me feel awkward, and so I slipped it into a drawer. But why should I have cared if my coworkers had noticed that I was reading Pascal? The name can hardly mean much to most of them, with the possible exception of Priestley. Whenever I see my colleagues on the train or sitting alone in the cafeteria, I observe that their own reading material is the stuff of the moment: government reports, popular novels, newspapers, nothing older than the decade. A copy of *Les Provinciales* was not going to spark any literary commentary among the staff, but I preferred to keep the book to myself—it seemed too personal for me to leave lying about. Anyway, I am apparently not the only member of the Foreign Service over here who conceals his reading. I seem to be in good company with no less eminent a figure than Ambassador Todd himself, a man not renowned for his devotion to the written word, who, rumor has it, a few days before he interviewed for his present post rather secretly went into seclusion with an entire year's worth of *New York Times*, trying to catch up on all the news he'd missed, and emerged after about seventy-two hours claiming to have had the flu. His wife joked with someone about the lost weekend, and then the anecdote made its rounds, and I'm pleased it trickled down to me, since I can be sure that my covert ways with printed matter would find sympathy in the highest of places.

Truly it's hard to fathom his reason for coming to Kovo on Friday. It's so unlike him; you mostly hear his name in the context of some lofty reception at the Embassy with persons of rank, or a splendorous social gathering. He seldom seems to budge from the capital except to fly to other capitals, and for him to suddenly announce that he's heading out to these remote provinces, in the dead of winter and with no evident cause, is very curious. One can only suppose that it's related to the troubles Kovo has lately seen, with all the harsh nationalist noise out on the street—the herds of agitators thronging the city square to chant their slogans, the history lessons barked out of bullhorns, the litany of ranting and roaring between the leaders and the led. Studying these crowds from the consulate windows, I can make out a lot of charmless young men united in their hate, whose rage, I expect, is the only pleasure they get out of life. One is naturally reluctant to deny anyone their bit of fun, and if the only consequence of their hatred were just the churning up of their own innards, one would not mind them getting on with it. But they wish to do actual damage, and have in fact done it, harassing the Jews who live in this city—a shrewd choice of victims, since nobody seems to care very much. The more refined forms of racism are well-established here—Jews are kept out of the better schools and the decent jobs—and the mass of bullies swarming the city square have been eager to do their part in this common effort, giving according to their abilities: smashed windows in the synagogue, broken gravestones, beatings, their violence becoming more and more wanton. The ambassador's visit may be connected to our having recently taken in a few frightened families who appeared at the consulate gates asking for refuge—if he even knows about their presence in our building, for Fitch has made it clear that they are with us unofficially. But even if he does know, would he really travel this long distance for a dozen downtrodden non-Americans? It would be out of all proportion.

And what about this book lying neglected in my hands—my last crack at bettering the day lost to mind drift? The breath of life in me has leaked away

23

in fits of inattention, for which I cannot blame Pascal. It is I who let those demons of distraction thwart me once again; they must be having a rollicking good laugh on my account. So, to bed—this Monday is done. I've put what finishing touches on it I could, made my last-minute attempts to improve the thing, grateful at least to have had a final go at it, and now it has to be abandoned in its quite imperfect state, to be judged by the Ancient of Days, or not judged at all— but that's not my concern.

TUESDAY

Early Morning

-You haven't touched your porridge, Jack.

-I didn't want it with raisins in it.

-Then I promise I won't give you another bowl. But you need to eat four bites. And two bites have to be with raisins.

-No, one bite.

-Then one bite with raisins and three without. Haven't you heard about people who don't eat their raisins?

-No.

-You haven't? Keep eating and I'll tell you.

-Tell me now.

-They grow whiskers.

-They do not.

-Well, have you ever seen a seal eating raisins? Or a cat? I haven't.

-Wait, Daddy—

-Eat two more bites and then tell me. Good, Jack—you're making me very happy. And if you eat your toast, too, I'll be so happy I'll smile.

-But some people don't eat raisins and they don't have whiskers.

-Like who?

-Mommy doesn't.

-That's because Mommy eats other things so she won't get whiskers.

-Like what?

-Like toast. And she never leaves her crusts, either.

27

-Daddy?

-Finish chewing. What?

-How many days is it till Mommy comes home?

-Not many. Yesterday there were six, so today there's only five.

-Five days is too long. I miss Mommy so much I wish I could see her right this second.

-I'll bet she's wishing just the same thing about you.

-Can we call her? Please!

-We can't because it's nighttime where Mommy is—she's sound asleep. But who do you think she's dreaming about—of all the people in the whole world?

-Me?

-That's what I think, too. Even when she's asleep she's loving you. And soon she'll wake up and say, "Only five more days until I see my Jack."

-Daddy, it's still yesterday in America, because people are sleeping when we wake up. And when they aren't sleeping we are. They're the opposite from us.

-Like when we stand up they sit down.

-Not that.

-Or when they're not eating toast we are.

-Not that!

-Let's go, Jack—last bite and you're done. We have boots to get on, and mittens and all our winter things. It's freezing cold outside. And your hair is a tangle - we can't send you off to school like that. Go get the comb for me.

-Why do we have to comb my hair every morning?

-Because every morning it needs it.

-But it hurts my head.

-Then I'll try to be gentle. Go ahead and get it—we have to be out the door in five minutes.

-I don't want to.

-Jack, I'm asking you to do something.

-Well, Mommy doesn't comb my hair every morning.

-Yes she does. And so do all the other mommies and daddies in your class. You ask the kids today.

-Sasha's mommy and daddy don't.

-Then I'll talk to them about it. Now let's not discuss it anymore. Go get the comb.

-Ivan's hair is never combed.

-Jack, do you hear me telling you what to do?

-But I don't need it!

-And I'm not going to tell you again.

-Daddy, you don't understand. Mommy doesn't do it every day.

-Then we'll ask Mommy when she comes home. Now I do not want to have to get that comb myself.

-You can't tell me what to do all the time!

-Alright, Jack, I'll get it. As soon as dinner's done tonight, you're going to bed. Now stand still.

-You don't understand anything I say!

-Don't move!

*

Mid-morning

I feel sluggish and dimwitted today. I'm a laggardly presence in the office, out of step and useless. Did I really come to work thinking that things would be normal around here? After the alarmists had sounded their sirens yesterday, I honestly expected that the excitement would quiet down, and we would all carry on more or less as usual, those in need of bracing themselves for Friday's guest doing so without greatly hindering the rest of us. Naturally one would want to spruce the place up before his arrival, replace the burned-out light bulbs and so forth, but since we don't even know why he's coming, I assumed there was little else to do except wait for him to show up. However, I seem to be the only one of us who's had any notion of doing nothing special, a realization I began to make first thing today on my way to the lunch room, when I passed a cluster of my colleagues who were heatedly discussing some crates of files in the basement. "Coffee, anyone?" I asked a shade too brightly, an offer no one bothered to make the slightest response to. Indeed, throughout most of the morning I have been largely unacknowledged by the staff around me, as they hold their pow-wows and proceed about the business of preparation, while I sit impassively over the same papers that occupy me day after day, not wishing in the least to be whirled around in this flurry of activity—and yet feeling oddly left behind. I guess I should do something to help the cause, but I don't know what. The most useful function at the moment would be to wipe that sense of purpose off of everyone's face; perhaps I could offer my services by dancing a jig or turning cartwheels through the conference room—some small contribution to make our working environment more relaxed.

It annoys me how affected I am by the mood

around here. The quality of my work today is no different than on any other day, but now it seems inadequate. I'm even smarting still from that non-exchange over the coffee earlier, and if such a slight as that could color my whole morning, then I'm truly a sad sack. I feel rather like a pouting child not included in some game. But why must every single event out of the ordinary be accompanied by an outbreak of edginess? Is it absolutely binding upon us all in these unusual circumstances to not be calm and to think of nothing but the event itself, so that oneself and the event become linked inexorably? Already this upcoming visit has the office in its thrall, and I fear that from now until Friday the staff is to be charged not only with the tasks deemed necessary to get the consulate ready, but also with committing itself body and soul to the occasion. Thanks, but there I must beg off. I'd really rather not join this juggernaut of urgency, and I take heart in the example set by Vermeer, an artist whose attention was forever being urgently demanded, by his debts and war and his children, fifteen of them, I believe, and you could forgive him for letting the strain of all that seep onto his canvasses, but instead his paintings are sublimely tranquil: a woman making lace, another standing by a window reading a letter, a milkmaid pouring from a jug. When he painted that lace maker, how much money did he owe? But who cares now? Time has washed away those debts, once so worrisome, and that war, whichever one it was, and left the woman leaning intently into her work.

I see that we're not the only ones today addressing an agenda—down in the square there's a rally of the malcontents in progress; from time to time you can hear them shouting out in unison. They too must be impatient to get on with whatever tasks they've set themselves, for otherwise why would they be outside on a bitter cold day like this, a lot of them with their shaved heads exposed to a biting wind? Don't they feel the chill? But then you wouldn't be likely to find a horde of menacing men all wrapped up in woolens, buffered against the elements by things knitted and cozy. On the whole these thugs seem quite impervious to the creature comforts, a hardiness that would be admirable if it weren't for the visceral emotion which appears to drive their cold away. But perhaps emotion is the wrong word here. Last week when I came into contact with two of these types on the train, they seemed dispossessed of feeling, reduced to primitive behavior that did not suggest any inner processing. When they boarded a few stops after me, one of them announced his entrance with an explosive stamp of his boot on the closing door, and I, who had been lost in a morning reverie, was jarred right out of my daydreaming; around the car there were a few gasps, but nobody said a word. The other one spat, splattering a window, and then they walked the length of the car and back, very slowly, looking over each of us as if they were prison guards, and when they sat down it was at the end of the car facing the commuters, opposite some poor woman, where they surveyed us without speaking.

If I was tempted to dismiss the episode as a case of ugly but harmless histrionics, I had only to recall that not long before, a pack of these men had acted on their impulses in one of these cars, throwing a teenage boy off a moving train, a Jew—one of their number had yanked the emergency cord and then they'd shoved the kid into the night, where he lay for hours until someone heard his groans. But our hood-lums were satisfied merely to intimidate us; after a couple of stops they got off, their brief, senseless hold on the passengers vanishing as others got on knowing nothing of the tension in the car. Only afterwards did it occur to me that this performance might have been their entire reason for being on the train. You couldn't imagine them travelling to an actual destination, and they certainly did succeed in having a brute kind of power over us, which in hindsight was ridiculous, for why would anyone want ten minutes of domination over a bunch of people going to work?

However, I have mostly been spared such brushes with barbarism. Up here we are removed from that kind of jungle mentality, and even though this rabble is visible from the consulate windows, we might as well be watching them on a television screen, so little do they seem to belong to our world. Their brand of anomie is alien to all the Americans here. Up in these quarters, anti-social conduct is taboo; we are kind or not to each other, considerate or not, but all of us have gone through the civilizing mill, and there at least we have something in common. And our world and theirs are eternally incompatible.

*

I must say this is what I call shabby treatment. I believe that I am being chastened, although it isn't entirely clear to me why. Perhaps my absence of alacrity this morning has been taken note of, and I've been quarantined in case my attitude is catching. But even if I did rather keep my distance from the swirl earlier, I wasn't unwilling to be pulled in, to do my bit without a grumble, and I hardly expected to be given a task that's emphatically menial, and given it by Priestley, who not so many months ago was my complete equal. Is there really nothing else I am able to do but sort through these meaningless files here in the basement, a job that could easily be done by a schoolchild? And I wonder how necessary it was for Priestley to mention twice Fitch's request that I make no decisions regarding the files, but merely put them in chronological order. I'm naturally grateful if he thinks I'm going deaf, but it appears instead that I am considered incapable of following instructions, likely to bungle the simplest of assignments through ineptitude or disobedience—some kind of oafish bolshevik. Obviously he doesn't believe that I have much to contribute to the ambassador's visit, and if my pride were not so piqued I'd congratulate him on his insight.

I am sorry about Priestley's condescending manner toward me. There is little affection between us, regrettably, really, for I had once imagined that we had it in us to be good friends. It was the attachment each of us had to books which made us seem likeminded, and in fact one of our first conversations was about the trial of Socrates, as I had seen Priestley, a newcomer like myself, at lunch one day reading the *Apology*. We discussed the merits of the Athenians' case against Socrates, somewhat self-consciously, I suppose, but we managed to mull the thing over without any obvious pretentiousness or ignorance, a feat for anyone. This exchange had pleased me, and I thought that here was a person one could actually pursue talk with, instead of retreating from it as I was often wont to do. However, we never did become companions. I myself tried to cultivate a friendship, and made the sorts of gestures one does to encourage a closer bond, thrusting my books upon him and inviting him over to visit us—indeed he was the first one from the consulate to see the just-born Jack, when we invited his family over for a visit—but it seems that he felt no strong affinity for me. He was less eager than I for discourse, and aloof, even, which puzzled me, since we were the only two around who showed any interest in the words that history offered up. He was even ambitious intellectually, and wrote essays on politics; and when he eventually got one published in some journal of international affairs, it caused a bit of excitement around the office: we had in our midst an authority on foreign policy. While I was giving his essay the obligatory once-over, skimming briskly along, I came across a reference to the *Apology*, and instead of recalling with pleasure the lively exchange we had had over it, I felt oddly disappointed: perhaps, then, he wasn't a common reader like me, but a professional one, his texts fitting squarely into the framework of his research, serving a practical purpose—Socrates himself deserving of Priestley's notice only because he strengthened Priestley's argument. And perhaps he, in turn, regarded me as a mere dabbler in ideas, content to meander among books while he was hewing out a path for himself, formulating a point of view which has congealed in other essays of his, something to do with *realpolitik*. I'm sure that he has classified me as an amateur, and quite rightly, too, and it's only a shame that he seems to have such a low opinion of them.

All of these moldering documents belong on

the garbage heap. They served their bureaucratic function a year or three or seven ago, and they'll never be needed for anything again, and anyway they are already in alphabetical order. Anyone who could cook up a job as senseless as rearranging this trash has a gift for making something out of nothing—maybe tomorrow they'll put me at the dumpster to separate tea leaves from pencil shavings. My only consolation is that there's work going on upstairs that's even more senseless than mine, and that's the planning of tasks like these. I couldn't forgive myself if I'd thought up one like this, so I guess there is some justice in my being down here, excluded from the company of my scheming peers—and even Caroline is up there having her say in the discussions, although you'd think a secretary's job was largely about just this, organizing papers. But Caroline is no less absorbed by the preparations than the others—her proper place is with them.

If I really am so useless around here, someone ought to inform those refugee Jews with whom I'm now sharing basement space. I am most unused to the deference I was shown when I happened upon their cramped living quarters on my way to this storage room. They all quickly rose to their feet, all thirteen or fourteen of them, the old, fragile people working to get up from their cots, a little boy being nudged by his mother. They seemed to view me as an eminently important official, some kind of plenipotentiary. "No, no, I'm only passing through," I protested, startled even to see them, since in my fit of annoyance at having been dispatched down here, I had forgotten about these frightened families. They maintained an expectant silence, having apparently lumped me together with the whole crew upstairs—all of us, they must have felt, being able to help them get to America or wherever it was they wanted to go. "I'm not in charge here," I told them in their own language, but this did not seem to diminish their reverence for me; on hearing their native tongue, men stepped forward to clutch my hand, while behind them broke the plaintive voices of women. But after having accepted a few effusive handshakes, I excused myself from the room, as it was pointless for me to stay and raise their hopes. The refugees are in here at Fitch's pleasure, and Fitch, I'm sure, would not be more likely to offer them his assistance if their advocate were I.

These uprooted Jews are an uncouth sort of folk, flabby in their ill-fitting clothes, smelling of onions and other unpleasant odors, with rotten teeth and bad eyes; one squat man advanced on me wearing bottle-thick smudged glasses crooked on his face. Next to the door I had come through was a row of misshapen, battered boots, the children's and adults alike looking faded and swollen, as if they were afflicted with elephantiasis. It was footwear suited only for trudging in—all except for a petite, polished pair amidst the deformed ones. But it wasn't only the pitiful state of these boots that I noticed, but also how neatly arranged they were, stretching in a tidy line along the baseboard, the sense of order seeming to restore to each pair a shred of worth which alone it would have lacked. The reduced circumstances of these refugees must leave them with the barest means of asserting their dignity.

*

A lunchtime walk

This day is having its way with me. The slightest of pinpricks to my pride has managed to deflate my spirits; I've sunk into a mood. The morning's feeble jabs are hardly the stuff of great emotion—being sent to sort through files? Inferring a certain tone in Priestley's voice? No one wanting coffee?!—but they have been enough to lay me low. It never does seem to be the fiercer thrusts which pierce me, the blunt, upfront attacks on one's character. Swords and daggers drawn I have parried; it's the veiled edges of daily life which penetrate. But what a silly thing a mood like this is. So childishly self-important, it won't make room for anything else in my mind, not even for my own child. I haven't given a single thought to Jack all morning, to my son, my poor boy who left the apartment in tears today. For the whole morning he might not have existed, and he, too, busy sounding out words in a book or having his lunch, has completely forgotten me and Ellen, and also his breakfasttime tantrum. For the bulk of our day we are oblivious of one another. And only towards evening will I return to him, as I return from something unreal, a dream or a play in which I have a part, and when I am with my son, the world will once again make sense to me.

Tonight I have to punish him, because I said I would. I have to remind him of his outburst, which by now is in his distant past, blotted out by a hundred other impressions, and send him to bed early. Is there no other solution? I want this evening to be for Jack like every other evening, a homecoming where home is love, and not just a time to face the harsh consequences of having been willful hours and hours before. For even in his stubbornness he is innocent. His naughtiness is natural, and yet it falls to me to correct it. I'm sorry, my child. This weekend I'll take him out; if it gets warmer, I'll bring him to this patch of river for a stroll and a mug of hot chocolate at that café up ahead, like we did as a family a few weeks ago. We had a lovely time then noticing all sorts of things together—the bridges, and there on the other bank St. Sophia's Cathedral, with its golden cupolas—which inspired a discussion between me and Jack about ecclesiastical architecture, namely about how churches here are built with domes while the ones we'd seen in Chicago have spires. And from there I managed to coax a simile out of him. "What do you think those domes look like?" I asked.

"My meringues," said Ellen.

"They have the shape of chocolate kisses," said Jack.

And we stopped to watch the river, that slowly rolling force flowing onward through the winter, yielding none of its onwardness—not even to the extreme cold of today, when ordinary forward motion requires something more than usual. This could be a baking hot August afternoon for all the river's current cares, and I can also see that it isn't troubled much by human concerns, not in the least registering my gloom, and not even aware that the ambassador himself may soon be looking down at it. It advances unaffected by all that overwhelms us.

Alongside this stretch of water, however, the few intrepid souls tread unsteadily, wisps at the mercy of the wind and air. I wouldn't be in this blast of weather myself if these doldrums of mine hadn't chased me out of doors; it's hard to sit still when I'm feeling down. Also, picturing myself at lunch with Priestley and Co. as they natter on about the efforts toward, anticipation of, or conjecture about The Visit makes the risk of getting frostbite out here quite the appealing alternative. Just imagining such a scene gives me a boost of warmth on my walk.

*

Afternoon

I have made a connection: I have matched a pair of boots to their owner. And absurdly, it has pleased me, as if the connection made were a reward for having been observant. I hadn't even noticed her at first, the woman to whom those well-polished boots must belong, the only ones in decent shape, but this time when I passed through the inhabited basement room, striding to my files in business-like fashion—trying to prevent another show of obeisance toward me—I caught a glimpse of her. She was a middle-aged woman nine or ten years my senior, hanging laundry on a clothesline. She met my glance briefly and then looked down, and maybe it was because of her slight figure that I linked her with that petite pair of boots, but there was some other quality I sensed for an instant, some trait that established a certain distance between her and her situation, and so distinguished her from the other refugees, whose desperation is naked on their faces and in their voices and even in their footwear. She hadn't made her presence known the first time I appeared in that room, nor did her expression when I saw her have any element of pleading in it, and indeed her only acknowledgment of me was that instead of shifting her glance from me back up to the clothesline above her, she looked down at nothing—if I'm willing to consider myself acknowledged by such a non-gesture. Her reluctance to betray any sign of distress may be the result of pride or shame or shyness, I really don't know, but it suggested to me the pair of boots free of any visible scuff marks.

My morning glumness has gone. In its place is a fragile lightness of spirit, the fruit of my lunchtime observations—and not only that of the woman and her boots. The goings-on upstairs have also been heartening to me. After my walk, as I went up to fetch an apple from my desk, I noticed that I am not the only one who's been given a menial task today; in fact, the office is positively teeming with menial task-doers. Caroline's cubicle is awash in her own files, and Larry Nolan is busy reshelving government tomes in the bookcase, and even Andrew Priestley, political seer at all other times, has been assigned to oversee the painting of the lobby. It seems that the real work of the consulate has been interrupted while all of us entrench ourselves in an early spring cleaning; and discovering that I haven't been deliberately excluded from anything of consequence up there makes me practically cheerful. Everyone's duties are as frivolous as mine—hurrah! So now I can have a grand time switching these files from alphabetical to chronological order, lark-happy in the knowledge that we're all wasting our time together, and since after all I'm on a par with everyone else, nothing should stand between

41

me and a state of bliss—nothing, that is, but the fact that soon these frothy feelings will go flat.

But I didn't choose the cheerfulness, or the gloom; they chose me. I wish I could cultivate a stoical indifference to these fickle moods, these superficial highs and lows which pose as real emotions. I would bar the door to them all. But I'm weak; when these petty impostors come knocking, I open up. I invite the goblins in and entertain them for as long as they like.

Why should this job of mine affect me in the way that it does? I care so little for it. I do my work without loving or hating it, and as for my colleagues, I expend no passion on them, either—not even on Fitch, with whom I seem to be psychically entangled. But as for violent feelings toward him personally, there is none of that, since there's nothing horrible about his behavior. He comes across as mostly middling, an ordinary creature consumed by the offices of a mid-level manager, and if he were not my boss but, say, my insurance agent, I'm sure we would be on completely reasonable terms. I would be satisfied with the service I received, and I might even be amused by the nervous attention he paid to the smallest of details. Here at the consulate, though, he is almost invariably the source of my shifting moods. He has a hold on my state of mind merely because I happen to rank directly under him in the chain of command. It's too bad that my career is of concern to me. If I could only treat it as a laughing matter, I would chuckle that grip of his loose.

It rather astonishes me now to recall that Fitch was another whom I had once envisaged a friendship with. My gregariousness apparently knew no bounds. But Fitch is a man not without certain accomplishments in the liberal arts, and these had led me to suppose him a person of some dimension. For one thing he's a good painter. Whenever he and his wife have invited the staff over, I have always been drawn to his watercolors hanging in their living room, landscapes of places the two of them have been to, a village in Spain, a Greek island. On my first visit to their apartment, he had guided me around his paintings, giving me a narrative of their travels, pleased, it seemed, by my interest in his artwork. And also on that occasion I had noticed a row of French classics on the mantelpiece, including my '*bien-aimé*' Pascal. These were his old college texts, his wife had told me as she made her rounds with a plate of appetizers; her husband had been an honors student and had even won some prize for translation. I found all this encouraging. It seemed to me that a person gifted in the humanities was likely to be humane, and in those early days I was hopeful of finding kindly company among the few Americans here, as I had just been sent overseas to this strange, far-removed region of the world. Initially, good will flowed between me and Fitch, and I developed an easy rapport with my co-workers. And also Jack had just been born, and no office worries kept me from being absorbed with my new son. It was a period of contentment in my life, although such periods seem to me greatly overestimated, since life asks more of one than merely to be content.

Gradually Fitch's goodwill toward me vanished. Or maybe it happened all at once, a year's worth of harmony gone discordant in a moment. I might have botched some project, unawares, and the news of it never quite reached me. But I would surely have known; documentation is a religion around here, and nothing fails to be registered on a piece of paper. If I had erred, my personnel file would have incriminated me. The fact is that my duties get fulfilled like everyone else's; like everyone else I meet the terms of my employment, and so there must be some other reason why Fitch has singled me out for his contempt—assuming it's not I who have singled him out as my imaginary adversary. I can't actually point to any incident which clearly betrays his aversion for me, and my strongest proof of it is in the accumulation itself of perceived displays of dislike. There was the time awhile ago when I saw a list of staff members on the photocopying machine—left there accidentally, no doubt—which had "Yes" written next to all of the names except mine and Hildebrand's, who has since left the Foreign Service. That caused me a couple of difficult hours. Where was my Yes? Hadn't my faithful service earned me even that teeny affirmation? And worst of all was finding myself alone in the same category as Hildebrand, that tired old lounger whom I had hardly seen do a scrap of work since I arrived. Was there no worthier soul with whom I could be Yesless? But I never did find out what that list was all about, and I didn't notice that I was deprived of any privilege granted to the others.

And then there is Fitch's custom of giving a card to each of his staff members on their birthdays—with the sole exception, as far as I can tell, of me. I did get one my first year, signed and stuck in my pigeon-hole, a bulk-order sort of card that I'd already seen propped up on others' desks, but then the next year and from then on the pigeon-hole yielded no birthday greetings—but this I can scarcely complain about, since there's a greater pleasure in not getting one from him. Ellen and I always mark the annual non-acknowledgment, and by now it's become such a tradition for us that I'd be sorry to see it end.

So on it goes, these irregularities adding up, and possibly adding up to nothing, and certainly to nothing of importance, but all the same I have invested myself heavily in trying to understand why it is that this particular man disapproves of me, since he's the one with the influence over my career. My career!—that weight on me, that encumbrance which I had once expected to adorn me, to lend luster to my person, but which now feels like a heavy hump, call it a golden hump, if you will. Once I thought such a fine profession would perfectly suit me; now I find myself disagreeably altered by it. It changes the way I relate to my world, causing me to distort the significance of success: pensions and promotions and prestige grow out of all measure, looming over me. I'm often tempted to lop that growth off—to chuck the job and return to the States to scrounge around for anything else—but then the thought of Jack always pulls me back. In order to rearrange my perspective on things—to turn Fitch into an insurance agent—I would have to uproot my family, a precious price to pay for my peace of mind.

Imagine my sharing these grumbles with the refugees on the other side of the basement. "I've got this boss I'd like to tell you about..." Disaffection like mine they would see as evidence that I was blessed: if nothing troubled me worse than this, existence could hardly get any softer. I wonder if they picture us as happy, we who haven't been hounded into hiding, who don't tremble for our survival. They must have felt humbled by me earlier because of how removed I seemed from creaturely wretchedness, being as I am a representative of this completely secure American race, well-fed and sheltered, and with grave matters of state to attend to; in short, a man of this world. It's really a shame if they think so ill of me. Perhaps I should make some sort of gesture to show them otherwise—let them know that we're all mortals here, appearances to the contrary, all of us having to face the same reckoning sooner or later.

I should at least find out if these folk are lacking in any of the necessities—food, for instance. We could all pitch in a few items from our shelves at home. Caroline might even be willing to organize the effort, as she's forever coming around to collect for office parties and the like. I'll have a word with one or two of the refugees to see if they could do with such a contribution. That woman with the polished boots: she would be the one to approach. It might be a little awkward, my making a beeline for this stranger in a room where I'm being watched intently, but think of those whose eyes would be on me: frightened, needy, unquestioning of my authority, less likely to find my action curious than to wonder if any good will come out of it for them. As for these files, their unity at the moment broken up into the alphabetical and the chronological, those two irreconcilable systems, they'll just have to wait until I come back to restore them to wholeness again.

*

-Forgive me for bothering you—I'm the one who came through here earlier—I work in the consulate. We know that it's hard for all of you here in this basement. If there are any urgent needs—water or food—if we could help in that way—

-Thank you.

-Is there anything that you don't have?

-No, we have most of what we need, thank you.

-So there's nothing? But what about...provisions? Food. Do you have enough?

-One of us goes out every few days to get food. The guards let us back in.

-So you don't need any?

-I don't think so.

-Well, alright then. And no one is sick—no one needs a doctor, or medicine?

-We're all more or less in good health, thank you.

-I had the impression...but I'm sorry, I must have misunderstood ... (This woman is actually rejecting me, as if it were I who wanted something from them, I who have plenty to give while they are destitute. How could she possibly not accept the little that I offer, when nothing is more obvious than their neediness? It didn't even occur to me that she might decline to be helped, and now I feel foolish standing here, my bounty spurned, the vast difference in our stations disappearing in her polite refusal of any kind of aid, and I really think I'm capable of walking off in a huff, and washing my hands of them all. So do without my help, woman, and good luck to you! My God, I take things personally. You would think that I was the wronged party here. Let's try to get back to the initial premise: They must be in need of some essentials, forget her avowal that they aren't, and I can provide them. This is still how matters stand, so why don't I just insist?

And yet: she has chosen to refuse me, and it would be unseemly of me to importune her. She is free to make such a choice, and I daresay it's the last scrap of freedom left to her) ...At any rate, it can't be easy for you all to live in such a crowded space down here.

-No, that's true. But we manage.

-You seem to manage very well. I've noticed how orderly things are.

-Can you imagine what it would be like if we didn't have order?

-I understand. You know, we're busy ourselves today creating order. We're expecting a visitor to the consulate, and so all of us are tidying up. That's how I've been occupying myself in that room next door.

-Really? You Americans are tidying?

-Is this a shocking idea? Are we known abroad as a disorderly and untidy people?

-No, but here at the consulate you are officials.

-Yes, but there's a more important official coming. He's turned us all into housekeepers.

-I'm sure you're joking.

-I assure you I'm not. It's only for a few days, though—and we certainly don't have to endure the conditions you do. This dark room, all the time.

-We're used to it. And we'd rather be here than in our own homes.

-It seems pretty awful to live in a basement like this. Quite honestly, it seems like a kind of prison. May I ask you why you decided to come here?

-We were afraid. Here we feel safer.

-Has there been any violence toward you?

-We were threatened. A few weeks ago someone came in the night and painted a message on the doors of all the Jewish families in our building. We

48

woke up to see in big red letters the word 'pogrom' and a date, December eighteen. We came here on the seventeenth.

-Did this happen only in your building, or everywhere? In the consulate we didn't hear anything about this incident, either before or after the eighteenth.

-We also didn't hear of any other threats. Maybe it was just a neighbor playing a cruel joke. We considered staying in our apartments, but...with the children.... And even if nothing did happen on that day, we would live in fear in our own homes. There was no one to protect us. So some families went to relatives in other parts of the city, and the rest of us came here.

-And you just abandoned everything, your apartments, your professions?

-Except for what we brought here.

-And even your jobs?

-What good is a job if you don't have a home? Anyway, they're firing Jews all over the city. There's no life for us here anymore.

-And yourself—did you leave a position?

-I worked in a school.

-Sir, my daughter is a musician. And we forgot to bring her music with us—we left behind hundreds of pages!

-Mama! We can always go back to get them. And I'm not a musician, I was only a music teacher in a primary school. We knew we'd have to give up our jobs sooner or later. For a long time we'd been expecting it.

-Well, with music you can begin again anywhere. I think you'll find that Bach will remain Bach even in a new world.

-Do you listen to music?

-With an amateur's ear.

-That means you love it.

-But I don't play; and I envy anyone who does. I'd like my son to start taking lessons soon. My wife wants him to study the piano, but I prefer the violin.

-How old is your son?

-He's five.

-With the violin you have to be patient. It takes time to make a good sound.

-Yes, but it's such a companionable instrument, with all those string quartets and symphonies, everyone playing together. You really participate.

-But the piano is not just for selfish virtuosos.

-Of course you're right. Probably it's just that I can't figure out how to get a piano up to our floor.... By the way, my name is Clark.

-Oh—I'm Dora.

-I'm sorry that for now you are deprived of music. I wish you a short separation from it.

-I wish that for myself, too.

-I'm planning to be down here tomorrow. Don't be afraid to ask for anything.

-I'll talk to the others.

-Alright.

*

Early Evening

-Come to the table, Jack—dinner's on. Come while it's still hot. Are your hands clean? No, they're filthy. Well, let's say grace and then you can wash them. Do you want to hold my hand? Dear Lord, we give you thanks for today, and for all the good things in it, and we ask you to take care of Mommy while she's far away, and Grandma. Amen. Go and wash now. When you get back I'll tell you about some people I met today.

What a strange sort of appreciation I feel for that woman I talked with this afternoon. She chose to keep silent about her troubles, and even more, to conceal them from me, as if by removing the veil from her sufferings she would give up the last vestige of her privacy. One is so accustomed to the airing of grievances, to the compulsive voicing of every kind of discomfort and discontent and distress, nothing standing between the sensation and the reaction, that actually refraining from complaint seems like the anomaly. Perhaps for certain of the beleaguered, such restraint is a final comfort: At least, they can say, I haven't yet displayed my misery.

-Are your hands clean?
-Yes. What were you going to tell me about some people?
-That I met some families today who live at my work—in the basement.
-They really live in the basement?
-They all eat and sleep together in one room down there—children and mothers and fathers.

51

-But why do they all live in one room?

-Because they didn't want to live in their own homes anymore. People were being mean to them there.

-Why were they being mean?

-Do you remember when we read about David and Goliath, how David was Jewish? These people are Jewish too. And they were living in apartments like ours, and had neighbors, too, like we do. But some of their neighbors weren't nice to them, just because they were Jewish, and they even wanted to hurt these families. So the families came to our basement to be safe, and no one bothers them there.

-But how did the neighbors know they were Jewish?

-I'm not really sure. Sometimes people have Jewish names.

-But were the Jewish people mean to their neighbors?

-No. But their neighbors decided not to like them anyway.

-I'm glad our neighbors like us.

-Yes, we're lucky we have friendly ones.

-Daddy, can we invite some of our neighbors to visit us?

-Probably not.

-Why?

-Because if we did they'd see that the little boy who lives here leaves all of his dinner on his plate. And then they'd make a rumpus!

-No, Daddy, really. Can we?

-Maybe sometime. Let's practice eating in case they ever come.

-I'm not hungry.

-This is it for today, Jack. Do you remember I told you this morning that you'd have to go to bed after dinner? So if you're all done eating, you can go get your pajamas on.

-Aaaawww!

-Do you remember what a fuss you made over my combing your hair? That wasn't a way to act.

-But Daddy, can't I even have a story? Just one. If you say yes, I promise I'll go to bed right after.

-Not tonight, Jack, I'm sorry.

-Aaaawww!

-But dinner's not over until you're finished eating—and talking, too, since at dinner you do both. If I were you, I'd keep on taking bites and thinking of things to say. And then you can have fruit, and when you've run out of things to talk about, you can just think of some more. You might never go to bed.

-Never ever?

-Well at least not for another twenty minutes. And the best way to make dinner last for a long time is to not chew and talk at the same time. I know one little boy who was a same-time chewer and talker— he'd get done so fast that he'd be in bed before he swallowed. Use your fork, Jack, and not your fingers.

*

WEDNESDAY

Predawn: a sudden waking

O my life O God O why have I forsaken you—My life squandered—My single passage through existence wasted on paltry anxieties—Money Things My appetites How I'm perceived—O forgive me for being so utterly unaware—So unmindful of the mystery of my being here—A creature on a planet hurtling through a universe—The only creature in the universe who is myself—Alive this once and taking it for granted—Persuading myself that reality is routine—O the madness of normalcy—Making conversation Sitting in chairs Reading magazines—Regulating my life around projects and schedules as if I were not subject to a permanent blotting out—Dear God I have failed to be myself—Failed to acknowledge you—I've accepted reality as being merely the behavior of my species—O if that's all there is birth behavior death— If there is only the surface—Despair—There's no hope unless what is obvious is unreal—All of it unreal—The stars and planets and gravity and human norms—The more obvious the more unreal— Skyscrapers and presidents unreal—Do not let me commit my only self to this image-world—Help me to live in opposition to it

*

I'm awake. Consciousness has come, bringing with it Me; then morning—but here there's a pause. The usual data which attaches me to what is outside of me is missing, so that I am conscious of myself but not in connection with anything. For a precious moment I might have any identity. But here the data comes rushing in, and more of it than I would wish for: the consulate, Ambassador Todd, the files, Fitch, Ellen not here. The Jews. These then are the particulars that today I am bound to; it is in relation to them that I will be a person today, however little inclined toward any of them I may be. For that instant, though, all of the associations could have been different—and I might well have liked another set far less.

There is something in my morning from which I recoil slightly. Which one of these entities is it? Ah yes: The Jews. I resolved last night that I would gather up some food for them after all, and so today there's the task of making an appeal to my colleagues. Overnight the asking has become a burden, and I'd rather not do it, but once one decides to be charitable, changing one's mind seems an act of uncharity in itself. What will Fitch and Priestley et al think of me for cadging canned goods off of them to offer to a bunch of lumpen natives? I don't look forward to raising the subject, especially in such hectic times as these, but then if I just didn't quite get around to mentioning the foodstuff, it really would be my fear of looking foolish keeping me silent. I'll seize my chance this morning, undoubtedly pleasing Fitch to no end: Todd will be here in two days, and my main concern is getting dusty cans of beets and sweet corn to foreign strangers. Now if this were an official giving campaign, a Project Hope, if we could present to the ambassador an organizational chart detailing the collection and distribution of the comestibles, and every additional can of proffered peas would delight him that much more, I would be quite the mastermind around the consulate. But alas! time is short, and the peas will have to serve as mere nourishment, containing no symbolic value whatsoever. This would not, I think, put me at odds with the ambassador himself, whose well-fed appearance suggests that he would have no argument with peas *qua* peas, and would readily dispense with any of their metaphysical properties. Eating and drinking seem to be very much part of his portfolio, and in this respect he does not shirk his duty; reports of him more often than not place him at a luncheon or banquet, being fêted or fêting others— he has, I believe, grown fat representing his country. And it is this gourmand who has us all in a tizzy, this unserious man forever grinning into cameras, as if smiling were indispensable in diplomacy. Is this a man to quail before? Think of him now two time zones away snoring in a bed, just a body needing sleep, as yet unsummoned to be the ambassador. It is this huffing body that our entire day will be devoted to. I would far prefer to spend today in bed myself, in recumbent retreat from the manic preparations, but the thought of it is too tempting to entertain. I am attached this day to the files and to Fitch and to the Jews.

*

Mid-morning

Whether or not one agrees with Andrew Priestley's assessment of international affairs, on one matter there can be no gainsaying him: he sure does know how to refurbish a room. He moves about the consulate lobby sanding woodwork and spackling patches of wall as naturally as he sits behind a desk, and he gives orders like the foreman of a construction crew: Go spread these drop cloths. You guys take a putty knife and scrape away the peeling paint. I had no idea he was such a handyman, and I find his expertise a bit daunting, since I can do little more with a brush or roller than slop the paint on, splattering everywhere. Instruments of building and renovating hang heavily in my hands, and I suggested as much to Fitch this morning when he pulled me off the files and reassigned me to Priestley's detail, although I think Fitch assumed that I was trying to avoid hard work. I said to him, "I'm a very unskilled laborer," to which he replied, "Right at the minute we don't need skills, we need labor. All of us have to sweat a little if we're going to be ready on time."

It seems that the appearance of our interior has overnight become an urgent priority—Fitch has had nightmares, perhaps, of crumbling plaster and a snowfall of paintflakes—and so rather than working leisurely in the musty silence of the basement today, useless in a calm, unhurried way, I find my bumbling self thrust into the buzz of activity. Here the air is thick with purpose, what little talk there is having a purely functional significance—instructions are given and assignments clarified—and there is no occasion at all for offhand remarks, so often the only kind worth making. Priestley seems to thrive in this environment, so energetic and precise is he, while undertakings as practical and pressing as this one make me wilt; I feel quite out of my element here, and would like only to curl up on some sofa with a book. Priestley would be astonished to learn that his simple commands deflate me, for they are not unkind or rough, but quite free of any show of attitude, the command itself being of far greater importance than the parties on either end, and when he tells me to go wash out some brushes or get started on a new wall, he gives the impression that his mind is blank at that moment but for brushes and wall and, of course, the finished look of the room. He reminds me of Jack doing an art project at home, the boy completely absorbed in assembling his seashells and buttons and beads, and requiring my presence only to find the glue or cut some cardboard—the difference being that Jack's play seems infinitely more valuable than Priestley's work.

I'm not sure which I like less: Priestley's lack of any personal element in conveying instructions, or the opposite: Fitch's compulsive manner of charging the space he moves in with indefinable personal feeling. I suppose that one would rather be unacknowledged á la Andrew, and grudgingly I've got to admit the utility of Priestley's unadorned directives, since after all a room is getting painted. On the whole he accomplishes things, and if you might wish he were less authoritative, still you'd be likely to trust him to formulate your foreign policy and also to apply a good coat of latex. He really is the figure of authority around here, even more so than Fitch, for his intelligence is much respected, and his judgments about consulate matters carry a sacerdotal kind of influence.

In fact, it was his voice of reason that held out during the last crisis around here, a year or so ago, when our security guards caught some skinheads lobbing bricks with swastikas painted on them through our windows, and arrested the young men, tossing them handcuffed into the basement. While Fitch fumed at everyone who might take a share of the blame—at the guards for not simply chasing the punks away, at the ambassador for not giving us safer facilities, at Caroline for telling a secretary at the Embassy about it, since now it couldn't be hushed up—and while the staff heatedly discussed all the options we had for dealing with this herd of mischief-makers, Priestley made the cool suggestion that it was in our interests to release these men immediately and with full impunity. We listened; he elaborated: the issue was not one of right or wrong, but rather of what decision would serve the Foreign Service best, since we were not simply some freewheeling agency. Ultimately, he stated, we represented the United States, and if we were to entangle ourselves in seeking our own version of justice ... One sensed the layers of learning behind his remarks; he spoke plainly enough, but it was understood that he drew on his reservoir of knowledge, and in challenging his perspective one was sure to get in over one's head. You could just imagine a slew of historical names suddenly raining down on you—Bismarck, Richelieu, Talleyrand, Machiavelli—and when a couple of us spoke up for making an example of the miscreants in the basement, we had little more than our gut feelings to go on, and these did not carry the day. The skinheads were released without a word of warning or reproach, and if you considered only the fact that they no longer directed their animosity toward us, then it was fair to say that Priestley's solution had been justified.

Well, just as I expected, I've managed to splash this paint everywhere, on my shoes, the floor, the windows. In my hands the viscous liquid seems to acquire a centrifugal force, flying off in all directions except onto the wall itself, on which I've made so little progress that it's like a work of art, the streaky unevenness my personal statement. I may be summoned later to provide an interpretation of it or, failing that, to explain why I've done so damn little so badly, when all around me everyone is intent upon getting things done, and Fitch is constantly popping in with his checklist, and the ever helpful Caroline is carrying supplies to the lobby, remaining chipper even as she lugs those gallon cans of paint to us, and the consulate is rapidly being transformed into a clean, bright, orderly workplace. And is it in the midst of these fits of single-mindedness that I propose to initiate a food drive, to stroll around interrupting labor in order to elucidate the plight of some families in our basement? I must be out of my mind. In the peace of my own home it seemed like a normal sort of gesture, a regular office collection, but here, now, it would seem surreal; Fitch would treat such a request as a mutinous disregard of duty. Others would be baffled or disdainful. Perhaps then I could ask Caroline to do a whip-round for me. She often makes little gestures herself, decorating the office on holidays, sending cards when one of us is sick. Mild and sweet at all times, she would not be scornful of this diversion of mine.

But I can't skulk about trying to avoid all the sterner types, and direct my appeal only to a soft heart like Caroline's. I hope I'm not as cowardly as that. O,

63

this was an ill-conceived idea, and I will fail to fulfill it. Those Jewish families won't get any food from us, since this is not a giving time and I don't have the nerve to make it one. My fear of looking foolish will after all keep me silent, thus making my uselessness upstairs and down complete.

Many times I've wondered at this ease with which others can be useful, fitting smoothly in, while I flop my feckless self about to no avail. Caroline, for example, who like me knows nothing about painting a room, still seems a necessary part of the proceedings, fetching things and cleaning up, not at all discomfited by her lack of know-how, cheerfully willing to pitch in where she can. If she were to be assigned the task of collecting food for the Jews down below, I imagine the basement would soon look like a farmer's market; she would cajole and keep after us in her lightsome manner until she had crates full of anything she wanted. If she were in charge of these families, they would think that God had sent one of his seraphim in the form of a woman, pleasing in appearance, who was determined to provide for their every need. Maybe next week, then, when all this hoo-ha passes, I'll raise the subject with Caroline. She really could do more for them than I could.

But didn't I tell Dora that I would be down there today, ready to be of service to them? They might be expecting me—they might have made out a list of things for me to get, dietary requirements, toiletries, every man woman and child with a bevy of special requests; a crush of needy bodies pressing in on me, exclaiming, entreating. I should not have involved myself, at least not in the guise of a consulate staff member on duty. I don't think I would have, had

64

that woman not stirred something in me; but somehow now those stirrings seem a kind of weakness which perhaps I should have fortified myself against.

*

The Basement

-Good morning. We weren't sure if you'd be passing through here today.

-I've only come down for a minute. I've been given a new job upstairs—can you guess what it is?

-I can see that you have paint in your hair.

-Right. Didn't I tell you yesterday that our only goal is to make this place presentable? You didn't believe me.

-I was just surprised.

-Not as surprised as I was when they handed me a paintbrush. I hadn't used one for ten years. And even back then I was hopeless.

-Maybe we could help you. I'm sure all the men with us do that kind of work. They'd be very grateful to have some way to keep themselves busy.

-That's a good idea—but we've just finished painting.

-Then maybe there's something else that we can do. We have a plumber here, and a carpenter. My sister-in-law makes curtains—

-Thank you. I don't think the building needs any immediate repairs, but if I'm wrong I'll let you know.

65

-So now it's your turn to refuse our offer. This is not in retaliation, I assume.

-Not at all. Actually, I did come down to see if you had changed your mind since yesterday. Maybe there's something after all that one of you needs?

-Our only need now is help in getting to the United States. But I'm glad that you decided to visit us. My mother wanted you to have a couple of small gifts.

-Gifts? Why?

-She appreciates your kindness to us.

-But I haven't done anything.

-Apparently she doesn't agree with you. Here is a pair of earrings for your wife. And this little flute is for your son—a start to his musical career.

-Really, this is unnecessary. I certainly haven't earned it. But thank you—and thanks to your mother. I'm afraid I can't give these to my wife until this weekend—she's in Chicago. But my son will be very pleased —in fact, I told him about all of you yesterday.

-You did? I wonder what you said about us.

-I tried to explain to him how you came to be here.

-I hope you didn't make us sound like victims.

-Why not? Aren't you?

-That's not how I prefer to think of myself.

-I see no shame in the word. Violent people have forced you to leave your home. You have a right to call yourself a victim.

-Am I required to enjoy all of my rights? I'd rather not be an object of pity, as victims usually are.

-I think you can be sure, Dora, that there is very little pity being shown to you right now. If there were more, you'd be living safely in your own homes, or in America.

-Maybe—but people can be kind without feeling sorry for us.

-Then you'll be happy to know that my five-year-old son didn't feel sorry for you. It was himself he pitied, since I sent him to bed early last night—and worst of all, without his bedtime story.

-What did the boy do to deserve such punishment?

-He wouldn't listen to his father.

-You should be gentle with him—if he misbehaves, it may be that he misses his mother.

-He does, it's true. Still, is it only during the happy times that we ought to act properly?

-What a strict father you must be!

-My wife tells me the same. However, you'll have to save your critique of my child-rearing tactics for another occasion. My colleagues are doing all the cleaning up upstairs.

-Of course. I'm sorry if I've wasted your time.

-You haven't. In fact, before I go—I'd like to do something for you later—or let's say for your mother. You wouldn't forbid me to do your mother a favor, would you?

-How could I?

-She said yesterday that you left all of your music back at your apartment. Is that right?

-Yes.

-But I think it must be necessary to you. When I have some free time, I'd like to go get it.

-My mother shouldn't have spoken out like that. I can't ask you to do that for me.

-It's not for you, it's for your mother. Call it an exchange of gifts.

-But my mother didn't expect anything in

return for what she gave you!

-And I also don't expect anything. Dora—this is a very easy thing for me to do. It's only a simple errand, and besides, I often go out at lunchtime. Just yesterday I went for a walk along the river. Do you live far from here?

-It's not far. About twenty minutes, on foot. But it's so much more than I could have asked.

-And it's much less than I could have done, believe me. I intended to do more. Listen: why don't you give me directions to your apartment and a key, and tell me where I can find the music, and when I can go I will.

-I'm obliged to you.

*

Lunchtime

Turn around this instant! Go back into the warmth. Call off this so-called errand, this foolish excursion to a destination you have no business going to. An errand! Errands are for stamps and aspirin— they don't entail anxiety, concealment, uncertainty, risk. I should not have come out on this adventure. I let myself imagine it would be like a trip to the drug-store—nip out, pick up item, nip back in time for a sandwich and a bowl of soup. I let the human factor draw me in—again! And now instead of limiting myself to mere food-collection around the office— what was it I had against that innocent idea?—I'm on the street, a member of the Foreign Service, paying a sneaky visit to a private local home. Hastening onward guiltily, informing no one of my whereabouts, eager to do the furtive deed, get the papers and get back with them unobserved, I feel almost treasonous, and I am certain Fitch would view it so. Out here on this midday mission I am acutely aware of myself as an American official, my identity interchangeable with my job title, a frame of mind that's most unfamiliar to me, since inside the consulate I seem to define myself by the very distance I feel from my official role. So is it only in striding headlong away from the consulate that I am convinced I belong there? Am I out of place wherever I am? Why don't I just give up this reckless plan, go back to the soup and sandwich, go chat in the lunch room, and then get back to work just like everyone else? The human factor can wait its turn.

Onward anyway. Against all reasoning forward-bound, for I don't have the impetus to interrupt my step and will myself back. The folly of my scheme only makes me quicken my pace toward that apartment, my case of nerves impelling me on rather than restraining me. What I really ought to do is simmer down, since even if Fitch does find out, I see no outcome worse for me than more of his contempt, a pathogen to which I have built up some resistance. Perhaps my poor judgment would cost me a promotion. But it is the hiddenness of my movements which disrupts my calm, striking out secretly like this, as though secrecy were something foreign to my nature, when in truth there is no instinct more natural to me than concealment; indeed, I believe it is the only thing at which I have ever really succeeded. The better part of myself has always been undisclosed, and the worse part, too, and I have been a person few others could imagine, for hardly a soul has ever suspected the life in me so much at variance with my exterior, a life which has often been the very negation of my recognizable self. I think of a fierce dispute between me and Priestley, a heated quarrel about the Church, against which I had much to say, while he defended his beloved institution, but how could he have known that I was that very day prayerful, asking God to deliver me from a despair I was in, despair which had nothing to do with Priestley or our conversation or anything else that I could put a name to, but which had been ravaging me since I had woken up.He even called me irreligious for casting doubt on the Church's purposes, and I did not feel obliged to explain myself to him. Or I think of one late afternoon when I happened upon Caroline in her office, distraught, weeping at her desk when she thought no one was around, startling me when she looked up with her bright face gone smeary and awry, and since she could hardly pretend that nothing was wrong, she had her cry as I looked awkwardly around for a tissue, and then she told me she believed her marriage was breaking down. For an hour I tried to console her, all the while feeling elated over her misfortune, giddy at the misery of this chirpy, likable woman who was suffering while I was not, until she finally declared, "You have made me feel so much better." I did not let her know how good she had made me feel, although I was less jubilant soon after at the news that she had patched things up with her husband; she assured me I had been a great help.

When I think of what has been unsaid—when I think of just how little I have said—

And yet my hidden ways have not been stealthy.

I am not one to pursue an unrevealed agenda, operating craftily in the shadows; and yet this expedition of mine does rather smack of surreptitious doings. Do I have an agenda unrevealed even to myself? I'm off to fetch for a woman a stack of her sheet music—what ulterior motive could I have?

She was wearing fragrance earlier, when I went down. I sensed about her a lilac aroma, the room redolent of purple perfume instead of yesterday's cooked onion. And her eyes, which yesterday had looked away from me, were less ashamed today. "We weren't sure if you'd be passing through," she had said. O it's that dance, is it? A *pas de deux* in circumstances such as these would be absurd. Perhaps she simply puts on scent as she would her elegant boots or a pair of earrings, as a matter of habit. Perhaps. She is not an unattractive woman. I could see that she had once had fine features. Have I been drawn into making this excursion because of her lilac scent and the vestiges of her beauty? Was it a glance from her which determined me to be kind and come out in this midday freeze? I don't know. My motives are obscure to me, and it may be that my impulse to help her was altogether other than it seemed. Or maybe it was just pity after all.

I know this neighborhood well. These are the environs Ellen and I had hoped to live in, this part of the old town with its churches hundreds of years old, and plaques beside doorways announcing the birthplace of a scientist or a poet. Six years ago we had first strolled on this narrow, winding street, down to the river where barges have carried freight for a thousand years. I would have envied the Jews their being established in this historic sector of the city. How charming to dwell amidst these ancient stones and domes, I might have said to them. Quite. That must be their building catty-corner. It's an elegant structure, with intricate designs in the masonry and cornices, and arched window openings, just the sort of residence Ellen and I would have noticed, wishing there were room in it for us. Now there is, quash the thought. Six years ago I must have imagined that the life one would lead behind such a facade would be dignified like the facade itself. Only noble spirits need apply. But entering now with the intention of ferreting through papers in an abandoned apartment, I feel anything but dignified. What if I'm observed snooping about, and suspected of ransacking the place? Who would believe that I've come for Chopin's nocturnes? And if I did explain myself, I would have to reveal the Jews' hiding place. I'd very much like to get this over with quickly. The emptiness of this corridor is not suggestive to me of peace, although once Dora's playing would have been audible out here. She said that the music is on the shelf behind the piano. So locate piano, then shelf, take music, go. O on the door—the red on the door—there it is—POGROM 18-12—the red paint scrubbed but still visible. What a menacing sight, the letters painted on in big, rough strokes, droplets streaking down to the floor. You couldn't come home to that every day and still call it home. Let's not linger here. Open the door, locate piano, then shelf, take—O Christ what do I see?

Could this be Dora's home? This where she lived? Is that her piano? My God what a stench. I can hardly breathe in here.

They carried out their threat. They attacked even without any victims. They've turned a family's home into rubble. There's nothing here but destruc-

72

tion and the overwhelming stink of human excrement.

They've demolished the piano. The upright has been overturned and hacked at, dampers and hammers pulled out, keys smashed. The floor is littered with shards of black and white. If there were any sheets of music for me to grab and flee with—but all the papers that I see are now confetti, ripped up and strewn across the living room. They have smeared their own feces on the wall.

If I stay here any longer I'm going to retch, anywhere would do, for this apartment already looks like it has vomited its contents, every object first chewed thoroughly up. Nothing is not in pieces, chairs, drawers, paintings, lamps, glass, clothes, books. They've torn the bindings off the books.

All the things of value that they could have stolen they've destroyed. They could have done half the damage and still been certain they had wrecked the place.

A piece of a toilet seat. A slashed pillow. A child's slipper. A plant pot knocked over, soil spilling out. But where is the plant, and where is the child's other slipper?

PART TWO

Afternoon: the conference room

What a great heap of fruit Fitch has managed to obtain for us. In the dead of winter in a city that's bereft of any harvest yield, the sudden appearance of a basket brimming over with ripe peaches and plums and apricots and nectarines seems to defy nature. I doubt there's another like it for a hundred miles around, and Fitch won't say how he procured this plenty, this token of his appreciation, he tells us, for our hard work over the last couple of days. Amid a general stretching forth of hands toward the basket, however, if not in some quarters an outright lunging for it, I restrained myself. After what I had just been witness to, how could I dare partake so soon of such a pleasant summer feast? For some minutes I watched my colleagues digging in, disdainful of the feeding scene before me. But my eyes rested on the violet plums, Victoria plums they were, succulent and sweet, and I let myself imagine their delicious juice slaking my thirst. I reached for one, and then for another.

I can't deny that Fitch has it in him to be generous. I would if I could—it would simplify things to be cynical about his motives, believing him only to be buying our obedience with his pile of fruit. I'm certainly ready to think the worst of him. But his goodies have shown up on the conference table in quieter times than these—strudels his wife makes, catered lunches, cakes and pies. And every year or so he hosts a soup-to-nuts affair at his apartment, an occasion for which his wife spends half a week preparing, and both of them bustle about throughout the evening providing for their guests, not excluding me, whose glass Fitch tops up like everyone else's. It is in these moments of his largesse that I turn against myself for making such an adversary of him. Grateful to his staff this afternoon and liberal in his giving, attentive to the talk around the table, he seems a model of moderation, cordial, approachable even, and I am reminded of the few occasions over the years that he and I have enjoyed a near-companionship. Once we met by chance in the marketplace, and wandered through it together buying things; once in the office he asked me about the Chicago Cubs.

Today seems another of those rare reprieves from the well-established tension, and I'm half-inclined to take advantage of the apparent truce to tell him what I've just seen—to offer him an explanation for my absence from the consulate. He should know how utterly dependent the Jews are on us—on him, really, since their fate is in his hands. Would he understand? Would he tolerate my having mingled with the strangers in the basement and then gone out to one of their homes? He should know about the home. But even if he does indulge me my involvement with the refugees, how could I convey to him the horror of the sight so that he would comprehend the depth of their degradation? The terrible vision I would impress on him has first to pass through the dark forest of conversation, where my thoughts are constantly getting disoriented, losing their way in a tangle of obstructions: the choosing of words on one's feet, the presentation of one's personality, the image that one would re-create broken into puzzle-pieces of dialogue only possibly to be reassembled, tone of voice and manner of speaking and eye contact and gestures. "Joe, could I have a word with you?" I would begin, but not know how to take my next step without stumbling. Then how can I get my load—this picture of disaster—through the thick wood intact; how can I make the impact on Fitch that's been made on me? It's too bad I can't deliver a soliloquy to him, a monologue in which I could depict the catastrophe, undistracted by my interlocutor, stating precisely what I intended. For such a speech I think I would have to talk to him through a partition, as if we were prisoners in adjacent cells, or standing back-to-back with him like duelists. He might not warm to an arrangement of this sort.

Telling Dora and her mother, on the other hand, will be a simple matter, for instead of trying to stun them with the brunt of what I know, I will disturb them as little as I can, sparing them all of the graphic details. I have only to avoid shocking them.

We've eaten down to the bottom of the fruit basket, reducing the delectable mound to a scattering of fleshy pits on paper plates. Our tummies are fully sated. Now that we've dispatched the edible part of this meeting, it's back to the business of the consulate. Ambassador Todd will be here in less than forty-eight hours, we are reminded by Fitch. It is unknown at this time whether the ambassador is conducting his own countdown in hours rather than days, but one naturally hopes that he shares our sense of imminence about his visit, since if he didn't, if for instance he were only dimly aware of having something on this Friday in one of the provinces, while we in those selfsame provinces were already glued to the clock, anxiously charting the progress of the little hand, such inequity in expectation would not be flattering to us. I didn't think we had to worry any longer about the time running out, that we would coast through the next couple of days at peace with ourselves, free from any pressing concerns, since the consulate is now immaculate and all in a state of readiness—all except for the files in the basement suspended precariously between those two systems of classification. I assumed the fruit had ushered in a respite from our toils.

But once again I am out of step: Fitch insists that we have a host of questions to resolve in the little time remaining. There is, for example, the matter of greeting the ambassador when he arrives at the consulate. Should the whole staff form a welcoming party outside, arraying ourselves at the gates in a straight line? Or if that's too formal, perhaps in a gentler crescent indoors, or would it be more appropriate for us to look busy at our desks doing the work of the Foreign Service while Fitch goes out to meet him with a smaller group? If only our sage counsel were not at all sought, and Fitch could work through these difficulties without any need for a consensus among us, my gratitude to him would be bottomless; for in these discussions there is never any final word to be said, but every moment of silence that starts to flower must have a weed to choke it, and there is no thought so unpromising that it can't sprout into speech. When Stan Hillman suggested that standing outside in subzero weather just waiting for a car to pull up would make us miserably cold, and that a warm welcome was harder to extend when your teeth were chattering, we nodded our assent, since one was happy not to challenge the logic of the thermometer; and so that issue was settled, and if we were all to meet the ambassador then it would have to be indoors—but now here was Betty Cameron just wondering whether we could find out the temperature for Friday, and Larry Nolan just wondered if we could get bundled up really well, and now the talk was back outside, and I wondered if there was a room in hell reserved for conversations like this one, where only nothing could be said and had to be said *ad infinitum.*

"But if he's late we could be out there for ages." In such wise was yet another comment tendered, this time by myself, and it hardly mattered to me whether anybody paid me any mind—they didn't—but I wished only to register my voice in this paltry debate. Although by joining in the idle talk I could not then pooh-pooh it, I didn't prefer the alternative of keeping a resentful reserve. There's nothing very principled about brooding. Happily, however, there has been no clamor for more of my insights, and they do appear to be managing admirably without me, especially Betty Cameron, a woman whose excess of chatter makes me think she has a physiological condition—a gland that overproduces speech, a valve that doesn't shut the blather off, a kind of verbal reflux. It isn't pleasant to see a person in the prime of her years with a bad case of ramble-itis, a malady that one associates with the aged and the unhinged, where the mind's checks and balances fail and fall into disuse. The infirm at least have the excuse of infirmity for their thoughtless pitter-patter—like Ellen's sick mother, babbling out her days in a nursing home, her clouded mind shedding a steady drizzle of nonsense words which bear incessant witness to the death of her memory. Now she's one who has paid in hard coin for the right to ramble; it cost her her very sanity. I can hardly complain about having to tolerate Betty Cameron when Ellen may at this very moment be listening to her mother's gibberish, seeing the woman who gave her life and raised her to be a woman herself only capable of incoherent, anxiety-driven drivel.

I heard it myself the last time I was in Chicago, sitting beside her bed while she shot wild-eyed glances about the room, looking in vain for some object.— Where is my my my my satch Ive got to have it please Ive lost my skatch help me find it please please theyre going to ask me for it its their schedule I NEED IT O please it was sitting right here on the the schedule I think someone took it I think someone came right in I must see their schedule could you please bring my sla my sklatch to me now I want to have it now you dont understand what will happen you dont see you really do not see do you I cant believe you dont see I cant believe it was right here on the the the the the the the skedge—and on and on and on, this woman who had raised children and been educated, too, B.A., Loyola University, M.A., Roosevelt University, the diplomas still hanging in her empty house, formal guardians of a mind that has escaped their protection and vanished into darkness.

At last this meeting is finishing—a stroke of good luck, as I assumed it would just continue until one by one we collapsed, the last one of us still to be talking free to decide the question of where the ambassador will be met. But Fitch has gathered his papers and impatiently cleared his throat and launched into his peroration, which suggests that relief is near at hand. One would have preferred only that his concluding theme were not What's Left To Do, for that could expose us to More Discussion. For once, though, I am glad to see him getting himself tense over some silliness, since in his nervous absorption with buffing and polishing he looks quite unwilling to brook any interruption, hushing us all. There might be another five minutes of this sermon of his, followed by a litany with a congregation that must have its word, then a hymn in praise of the fruit we have received, and finally we will file out, reflecting on the lessons learned: let's say fifteen minutes in all. However, here is Fitch addressing a question to, of all people, me, staring expectantly at me across the long table while I hasten to look alert; and I am stammering and fumbling for an answer, an inadequate one that has dissatisfied him, and I am fumbling further, groping to explain why the files in the basement are not yet in order, but Fitch is suddenly possessed of the idea that the whole lower level is a shambles, the only area we've neglected, and the fingers on his fist are snapping to attention as he numbers the things to be done down there, starting with my own unfinished task, and then all those people have to be cleared out, after which we can prepare the whole floor for a possible inspection, tidying the storage closets and getting rid of the junk that's been piling up for years. That could take us to Friday morning, and with the ambassador due at eleven—

What I've just heard cannot be what he's said. I must have misunderstood him, or missed some clarifying fragment as I was dwelling on his displeasure toward me. There's surely an explanation. But Betty Cameron has heard the same thing, and while I'm made dumb by my bewilderment, she has cut him off mid-sentence. "What was that you said about the people downstairs, Joe? What are you planning to do with them?"

"They can't be around when the ambassador arrives. He doesn't know a thing."

"You mean they'll just be kicked out?" she said. "But you can't be seriously considering that, in weather like this."

"They can't stay here, Betty. Do you know what could happen to us if we're discovered hiding an entire roomful of aliens who aren't even authorized to be in the building? I'm talking about careers."

Caroline said, "Maybe it's not too late to let the Embassy know they're here, so there wouldn't be any surprises. I could call Jenny Larsen and tell her."

"No, it is too late. I don't want some last-minute mess screwing up the visit."

I spoke up. "Why don't we send them away just for the day? They could be out of here first thing Friday morning."

"I agree with Joe," Priestley said. "This is not a time for us to be harboring refugees. Whether or not the Jews in Kovo are being persecuted, no one has actually recognized the fact—not the State Department or the U.N.—not even any of the human rights organizations. Do we want to give the impression that we're some maverick outfit making up our own foreign policy?"

"Are you suggesting that Jews are not being persecuted?" I demanded.

Fitch interrupted. "Not a single one of the people downstairs has said they've been hurt by anybody. We interviewed them all. No one's laid a hand on them or on their property. They came to us because they were being threatened, but let's face it, here everyone gets threatened—it comes with living in a country that's falling apart. Did you all hear what happened to me two weeks ago, right in my apartment building? Three skinheads were in the elevator when I got on, and one of them started staring at me, all the way down—he must have been ten inches from my face.

84

We reached the ground floor and this punk suddenly blocked my way out—he planted himself right in the doorway—and asked me if I was an American. I said I was, at which point he looked at his pals—you know, as if confirming that he now had every right to bash my head in. Then he moved in very close to tell me that foreigners like us had better get out, and soon, if we knew what was good for us".

"My God, how frightening!" Caroline exclaimed. "What did you do?"

"What choice did I have? I listened to him while he menaced me, and then he and his buddies took off—but not before he sent the elevator back up to the top floor with me in it. And I haven't seen them since."

"But you could run into them any time," Caroline said. "I couldn't stand it!"

"So these Jews are basically in the same boat as the rest of us. We're all dealing with a threat, and if those families down there don't want any contact with that mob, I certainly can relate, but this consulate is not the place for them to hide in, especially not now."

"So instead these families have to go live on the street?" Betty asked.

"Who's talking about the street? They still have their homes, from what I understand. They chose to abandon them and they'll just have to go back."

I said, "But if somehow they had lost their homes—then they could stay here?"

Priestley reentered the discussion like a mediator separating two squabbling parties. "May I say a word at this stage? I think we're losing sight of the fundamental issue here. None of us wants these people to be threatened, or made homeless, or to suffer any kind of mistreatment. We all agree that they deserve to live safely in Kovo, and that no, they should not be out on the streets. The question is not about our personal feelings, though—it's about whether we should be the ones to secure the safety of these people, and it's clear to me that we'd be setting a foolish precedent by protecting them. The local police are hired to do just that, and if they fail in their duty, is the U.S. consulate supposed to pick up the slack? Should we start helping anyone in Kovo whose civil rights are being violated? You know, we're not a relief agency, but an intermediary between two countries. We act on orders from above, and both countries' governments would be outraged to find us making ad hoc decisions about matters in Kovo that don't concern us. If we're determined to do something, we could always set up a committee at some point to consider recommending that a certain number of visas be made available to the Jews in this city. It's the only real means we have of addressing the problem."

"This is no fun, folks," Fitch said. "But Andrew's right. We'd be asking for trouble by championing their cause at a time like this. Maybe I should have turned them away when they first showed up, so we wouldn't be having to sort this mess out now. But I think on Friday when the ambassador is walking through here and seeing what a first-rate operation we run, you'll realize that everything we did to get ready made sense. Caroline, I'm going to ask you and Stan to go down and talk to them. Stan can do the translating. Tell them we're sorry, but we can no longer shelter them—don't get into any reasons why. Explain that they need to be out by noon tomorrow. If they want transport back to their homes we'll provide it for them, but that's as much as we can do. Everybody else can go home and get some rest. We've had a long day."

*

After the meeting

-Joe, could I speak to you for a few minutes?

-What's up, Clark? I've got a hundred things to get done before I leave today.

-Yes, of course. I wasn't able to gather my thoughts at this meeting just now, but I'm concerned about the fate of the families downstairs. It seems to me very possible that they don't have a safe place to go from here.

-They've got their homes to go back to. That'll have to be safe enough.

-But let's say that for whatever reason their homes have become off-limits to them—so that like Betty said, they might really be facing the streets. If that were the case, would you consider letting them stay?

-Look, Clark, I made myself clear, if not to you then to everybody else. They can't keep on living here. I've given a lot more thought to this matter than you're aware of, and if you want to know the truth I've even lost sleep over it. Who wouldn't feel for them? But I based my decision on what's right for the consulate and for all of us in it, including you, and I'm afraid to say that what's right for us doesn't depend on the circumstances of these families.

-I see. Then I have a confession which might

87

make you change your mind. I know you're busy, Joe, but this won't take long. While I was in the basement yesterday I got to talking with one of the women living down there—I had to go through their quarters to get to the files. She told me what they had told you—that they had been threatened—but threatened with a pogrom, with being killed, and it was because of the children that they had decided to seek asylum. Anyway, this person I met happens to be a piano teacher, and it turned out that she had left all of her sheet music behind, at her home, and since like you I felt for these people and I wanted to do them some small service, I went to this woman's apartment at lunchtime today to get her music for her.

-You did what?

-I knew that it was foolish of me, and I can't justify it to you or even to myself. The idea was all mine and I'm sure that it was wrong. It wasn't far to the building, though, a fifteen-minute walk, and when I got there I discovered that some hoodlums had broken into her apartment. They'd wrecked the place. It was like a bomb had been dropped on it. The fact is, Joe, that she and her family don't have a home anymore, and that's why I'm asking you to let them stay.

-I can't believe what I'm hearing. You went to one of their houses? You just took it upon yourself to make a decision like that without consulting anybody?

-I hadn't been trying to arrogate any authority to myself. I simply meant to do this woman a small favor, and I never expected to see what I saw in that apartment.

-You had absolutely no right to concern yourself with the situation down there. It's a violation of this consulate's trust in you—and frankly, Clark, I've really had it this time. When the visit is over you can expect to hear from me.

-What do you mean—this time? You speak as if there's a pattern to my offering these people help. Before yesterday I had never met a single one of them.

-A pattern is exactly what there is—a pattern of behavior that's been going on for a long time—far too long. I should have addressed this problem a lot earlier, and then things wouldn't have gotten out of hand like they have.

-Wait a minute, what are you accusing me of? I've had the impression for quite awhile that whatever I do around here meets with your disapproval, but I've never understood why. Have I broken any of the rules? Am I not doing my job? What is this problem that needs to be addressed?

-Look, this is not the moment to be getting into that. You can plan on my dealing with this matter, and soon, but I've got other more important things to think about just now.

-Well I must say I'm curious to discover these shortcomings of mine that you're hinting at.

-You really want to know what it is? Then I'll tell you. It's your attitude. It's your indifference to the mission of this consulate. The rest of us work as a team, we exchange ideas, we give each other feedback and support, we're all part of a single network, and we function together—all of us except for you. You come in, put in your eight hours, and go home. I really don't know what makes you tick, but it sure isn't any sense of dedication to your job. You never ask your colleagues for assistance or show any interest in professional development. You don't join in even if it would help your consulate or, I might add, your country—

and this latest episode demonstrates that perfectly. Would you like to know what the rest of us were doing at lunchtime while you were out and about? We were working. Everyone but you understood without my having to say a word that there isn't time this week to take off—it was obvious.

      -I agree that I went off when I shouldn't have. Even as I did it I regretted it, and it couldn't have fit into a pattern of behavior as you say, since I've never done anything remotely like it before. I lost my head and I'll accept the consequences, but at the same time I ask you—I entreat you, Joe, this once—to grant my request. If you had seen that horrific sight, you would understand that these people have nowhere safe to go. I'm asking you to let them stay even for just a few days—if anyone finds out about their being here I'll take the full blame for it.

      -Let me be honest with you, Clark. After what I've heard from you today, I intend to reassess your performance here and also to determine your value to us for the future, and you're not doing yourself a favor by harping on this theme. If I were you I'd be trying hard to prove that my job meant something to me, and you can do that over the next two days by working like hell to help us. Now, I don't have another second to spend on discussing this—I won't be out of here until midnight as it is. If you want to be useful you can go through the lobby and make sure everything has been picked up from this morning—but don't touch any of the walls. And could you close the door behind you?

*

The basement

-Clark, there you are. Thank God.

-I can't stay, Dora. I'm not supposed to be down here.

-Have you heard? We're being forced to leave. We have only until noon tomorrow.

-I know.

-They wouldn't tell us why, they just said it was orders they were following. What has happened?

-It's the visitor I told you about. We're expecting the American ambassador on Friday. You have to go because of the fear upstairs that your being here could complicate the visit.

-So that's the reason. But couldn't the ambassador help us get to America?

-He doesn't know you've been living in our basement. It's been kept from him, and my boss is determined that he not find out. Apparently, it's easier to chase you away than to explain your presence here.

-But when the ambassador leaves—?

-I had the same thought. But I failed to get you any more time here. You won't be allowed back.

-I can barely imagine returning to that apartment. My child's life is in danger there.

-You have a child?

-That boy sitting with my mother.

-But when I spoke of my own son, you didn't say a word about yours.

-I didn't think to.

-Dora, I must tell you about your apartment. I went there this afternoon to get your music. They had come and broken in. They spared no violence—everything is destroyed. Your home is not a place to live in

91

anymore.

-O God!

-I'm sorry. I think they must have taken their revenge on you for not waiting until they could carry out their pogrom.

-We could have been in there. If we hadn't left when we did—O—I'm sorry. Please don't let my son see me like this.

-You wouldn't have been there when they came. You knew what was happening.

-We might have been. My mother wanted to stay.

-But you knew better than your mother. Now you don't have to go near the place again.

-But where can we go? This consulate is our only refuge.

-Is your husband here to discuss this with you?

-My husband and I are divorced. He no longer lives in Kovo.

-Then who in this city can give you shelter? Are there friends, relatives?

-Clark, we turned to the Americans because you were our last resort. Most of the other Jews in Kovo were smart enough to leave when it was still possible, including our relatives. Our friends—well, we have had more to ask of our friends than they have been able to give us.

-Have you asked any of them yet for a place to sleep?

-If the best of them stopped acknowledging us in public months ago, how likely is it that they'll offer us beds in their homes at great risk to themselves?

A silence ensues.

-In less than a day you will all be out on the street in the middle of winter. Maybe with the others you can think of a place to go, even for just a few nights until we can find something else for you. I'll come back in the morning as early as I can. In case you need to reach me, I'm giving you my telephone number. You can call me anytime, it doesn't matter what the hour is. I can't stay a moment longer, Dora.

-Go quickly.

-Listen. If you have nowhere to go tomorrow, I want you and your son and your mother to come to my apartment. You can stay with us.

-Thank you, Clark. If we need to, we'll accept your offer.

-Do you promise?

-I promise.

*

Evening

How do I sit so calmly rocking in this chair, singing Jack a gentle lullaby at day's end, when I am shot through with uncalm, distress inflaming every part of me? I could burst with disquiet, while Jack sinks into sleep at the sound of my murmuring, rock-abye voice, that same one he hears every night, the routine tonight the same as always: suppertime, story-time, bedtime, the normalcy of our evenings replaced merely by the pretence of normalcy, which Jack in his infinite innocence seems not to have noticed. Still, if

Ellen were here she could at least have animated the evening routine for him, leaving me to tend to this raw burning misery of mine which makes me want to hurl my body into feverish activity, pacing, striding, moving any which way just to cool the burning off. Even my prayers are instantly consumed in the furnace of my feelings.

I am tormented by the image of Fitch. I could curse him for being evil, or insane, a demon without a soul—or is it myself making a demon out of this ordinary man who just today came bearing gifts of fruit, this mandarin preoccupied by bureaucratic trifles? No one else thinks he's demonic, not Caroline, who acts upon his orders, or Priestley, gladly lending him his intellectual heft, not even Betty Cameron, bless her anyway for speaking up, who cornered Fitch after the meeting today to ask about attire on Friday. Only I, it seems, am being haunted by a vision of a hollow man, a creature rotted through, and if I'm wrong it must be that I'm prey to wild wanderings of the mind, twisting common features into ghastly ones, and if I'm right and Fitch is truly just a merciless husk of a man, then how can I possibly account for his reasonable demeanor? It's that very reasonableness which torments me—his horrifying decision so well wrapped in logic that one misses the horror for the rational justification of it. Who would have overcome today his potent blend of argument and authority? Not I, that's certain, and the mess of it I made in trying stabs me with remorse. Everything I said but shouldn't have or didn't say but should have sticks in me, most of all the moment when I found myself the object of his anger, and rather than making any effort to keep his attention on the plight of the Jews, I forgot them entirely to wallow in my own troubles. There was no one to plead for Dora's people but me, and no time to do it in but those few minutes that I had with Fitch, and when I might have been saying something that he just might have attended to, I was instead busy discussing my boss' low opinion of me, evidently a topic of such great importance that I could let nothing else interfere with it. And even what case I did make dismays me, my single chance to paint a graphic picture of that scene of desolation lost in a blurry sketch of some generic break-in, a garden-variety act of vandalism committed by a few of the local hoodlums—hoodlums!—the very use of the word a failure on my part, expressing as it did none of the fury of rabid human beasts unleashed. It was my own reasonable demeanor which did such a disservice to those families—they desperately needed someone to be unleashed in their defense, to advocate without restraint for them. I could have done more, and when I said goodbye to Dora earlier today, looking as I took my leave into that lovely face, her glance once more shifted downward away from me, and the now-recognizable movement which yesterday I had attributed to pride or shame might well today have been a gesture of reproach, she too suspecting what I knew—that I could have done more, and it was I who was ashamed.

What is happening in the basement as they await the morning? Even in their anguish they must be doing something, patching together some plan to save themselves, or not, perhaps just yielding to panic and despair, overwhelmed by the disaster that is upon them. Has their alarm crippled them, or are they even now packing their things, putting their children to sleep—God knows maybe even cleaning up the place?

There's no telling what one would encounter entering that room, and yet what does it matter whether they are suffering openly or making themselves useful: the anguish must be lodged in them like a malignant mass discovered on an organ, possibly not manifesting itself in any outward signs but in truth the very heart of reality.

THURSDAY

After midnight, sleeping and waking

Fitch is standing in a tiny room cluttered with glass and porcelain objects—he has a baseball bat—I am there, too, recoiling into a corner—he's stepping toward me, rearing back, sure to whack me—here it comes, I'm clenched against the wall, he's livid—glass is exploding and fragments of porcelain are whizzing by me, but somehow he has not landed his blow—Caroline and Betty are chatting in another corner of the room, unaware, it seems, of the bat and the shower of sharp objects—he's swinging again, and again, missing me, but if I dare untense my cowering body that bat is bound to connect—Caroline is looking our way, but her face is a blank.

I'm in danger of losing my job, there's no doubt in my mind. After yesterday, I don't even see how I'll manage to keep it. But what will we do? Money. We'll run out of it in a month, just getting back to the States and renting a place to live, and then all the incidentals of moving, and the security deposit will set us back hundreds. All the money that we don't have that we'll need. And then the benefits will disappear, health, pension. Jack and Ellen will have their stable lives disrupted, Jack taken abruptly out of school, and Ellen forced to make a strenuous move back home before being thrust into reduced circumstances, she as well as I suddenly faced with the problem of making ends meet. If I am fired it's my family that must be dragged through the aftermath, my wife and child who had no say when I set off for that apartment—it's my dependents who will pay for my independent action, and I can't even claim the moral high ground because of my muddled motives. That fragrance; her alluring reserve; the helplessness of an attractive woman.

I am face-to-face with a woman of exquisite beauty, a dark-haired Madonna in the flesh whom I am yearning to caress, whose gentle features fill me with awe. It must be that we're together, since she is standing directly opposite me, just inches away, and there is no one else nearby. However, her eyes are cast down and she will not raise them to me, and I don't know why—if she only would, if those heavy lids would lift and she would meet my gaze with hers, I am certain I would find there all that my heart desired, the tenderest, most loving expression, and meant for me alone. But she remains staring down, motionless, and although I am trembling, and tearful with hope, I begin to understand that I will not be granted even a fleeting exchange of glances.

How long have I been lying here awake? It must be well over an hour now, sleep unable to get a word in edgewise as a multitude of voices vies for my attention, the loudest, most insistent one demanding to know what's keeping me from just bringing the whole lot of them to my own apartment and letting them camp here until they find another place to go, half-a-dozen in the living room, three or four each in the dining room and Jack's bedroom. Those three rooms may be their last hiding place in Kovo, and there's floor space, at least, for everyone. I can't fathom how one explains to one's wife that while she was away one's home was turned into a shelter teeming with refugees; indeed, the thought of doing this to Ellen alarms me only slightly less than the expulsion itself from the consulate a few hours from now—but Ellen's return in two days is an event remote in time, an age away from twelve o'clock noon. The whole idea is of course utterly absurd, but what lies in wait for these people elsewhere makes such absurdity seem perfectly logical. If I can only silence until morning the sensible voices which would convince me of the lunacy of my scheme, I can get the Jews here and then give an open forum to all my doubts.

I am walking down a corridor to get to my desk, my briefcase crammed with papers, bulging files I've got to get through, an impossible amount of work. There's only one door at the end of the passageway, but entering the room, I don't see my desk anywhere. Instead I find myself in that demolished apartment, where the entire floor space is covered with debris. If there were just a corner for me to spread out my papers, I could still get started here, but this carpet of trash is so thick that there's no place I can even put down my briefcase, the weight of which is making my arm ache, and while I'm searching for a bare patch of floor a telephone starts ringing in the room, an urgent jarring summons, but where the apparatus is in all this chaos I don't know, and in my confusion I am fixed to my spot, intent on answering the phone but unable to move in any direction as it rings, and rings, and rings....

My God the telephone. Dora, don't hang up please don't hang up

-Hello?

-Clark, forgive me for calling at this hour.

-Dora, where are you?

-In a phone booth. We've left the consulate.

-In the middle of the night?

-It's almost dawn. We didn't want to wait until daytime, when we would be more noticeable on the streets.

-But what are you doing, where are you going?

-We're making our way to the synagogue. The rabbi is still in Kovo and he's given us permission to spend a few nights there, while we work out something else. Your invitation to me and my family was so kind—you have no idea how moved I was by it. But I couldn't leave the others now, especially the older ones who rely on us. They're my mother's cousins.

-You can bring them to my apartment, Dora. There's room for all of you here. It will be more crowded, but you'll be safer. The synagogue is a public place, and it's even been vandalized.

-O thank you, Clark. But there are just too many of us for a single home.

-Ordinarily, yes. But these are extreme circumstances.

-Yes, I know, and it's so hard to make decisions in them. The rabbi is expecting us. He's preparing a sleeping space, and everyone is very tired, not even the children have slept. Maybe tonight we should go there, just until we can get rested.

-Can you keep out of sight?

-I hope so. We'll be in the basement again. Clark, I must go now.

102

-Alright. Keep in touch if you can, Dora. Call me anytime.

-I'll try to phone in a day or two. I feel easier in my mind already, knowing we can turn to you. Goodbye for now.

*

Noon

At the consulate we are now in full possession of our final instructions for tomorrow's visit, all matters of dissension having been decisively resolved by Fitch, who, we are given to understand, pondered these matters last night until the early hours. His lucubrations have yielded a crisp memo, hand-delivered to us all by Caroline: in the morning everyone is to enter the building through the back doors instead of the front so as to avoid tracking mud and slush across the gleaming lobby floor; we are to proceed with our daily duties, not interrupting them even when the ambassador arrives, and will assemble only when we get word to and no later than lunch, when we will have the honor of seeing our visitor add to his substantial girth. The greeting party will consist of Fitch and Priestley, clearly the right choices as they are both utterly serious about making a good impression. Fitch has apparently become convinced over the course of this week that the ambassador is coming here with a view to filling some plum positions that are open in the Foreign Service—why otherwise would he be so reticent about his reason for making this trip?—and the prospect of promotion renders his visit sacrosanct. Up to the last minute we have been unstinting in our devotions: the doorknobs have been polished, the computer screens windexed, a thousand files put in order and every desk made tidy—including my own—stacks of paper stuffed into my drawer, hidden away underneath the volume of Pascal. Every trace of habitation in the basement has been removed, even the clothesline that Dora was standing at when I first noticed her. Indeed, the Jews might never have been here but for a faint odor of cooking, the only remnant of their stay the smell of boiled cabbage—but I do not doubt that my colleagues will take whatever steps are required to prevent it from lingering. The Israelites who long ago fled Pharaoh's Egypt must also have left behind them a slight aroma, that of hastily-baked unrisen bread, bland necessary nourishment just like the vegetables in the basement. Has nothing, then, changed in three thousand years? Yes, maybe—maybe they didn't eat cabbage back then. Jewish cooking is not just the latkes and gefilte fish and the haroset at the Seder table, but also the meals made in a hurry, the flavorless food meant only to sustain a family in flight. Dora's last meal here was no less Jewish than any kosher fare.

Now all those lumpy boots are lined up neatly in another shelter, catastrophe averted for the time being. No one at the consulate has any idea where the basement-dwellers took themselves in the night, and I have not felt inclined to enlighten them; in fact, I can hardly bring myself to speak to anyone around here today. After what has occurred, the briefest communication relating to this visit seems to me an act of

104

betrayal to Dora, even a kind of profanity, and when Caroline came around earlier to inspect the cubicles, she found me so withdrawn as to appear ill. I expected her to reproach me for sitting at my desk doodling on paperwork while everyone else was still pitching in, but instead she was her usual solicitous self. "You don't look very well, Clark. Is there anything the matter?"

I said, "Actually, yes. I'm disturbed about what's happened to those families."

On hearing this, her demeanor changed completely: the clipboard poised on her hip fell slack, and a soft wail escaped her. "Do you know I went home last night and cried—I felt so bad for them." Her air of industry quite gone, she stepped into my cubicle and leaned toward me, whispering, "I'll be so glad when this visit is over." She seemed perfectly allied to me in my dejection, which astonished me—here was really a kindred spirit when I had thought there was none! The relief of it lifted me to my feet.

But it was Caroline herself who had served the Jews their notice to leave. She had obeyed that command. I looked into her agitated eyes and saw clearly enough that the incident had made her miserable, as it surely must have, since she is by nature friendly and good-tempered, and when not naturally so then willfully determined, even under duress, to project unflappable cheer. You could count on Caroline for bonhomie—but not for questioning the order of things, or for taking a stand. I said to her, "We certainly have shamed ourselves," and even this muttered comment had more controversy in it than she could accept; her troubled countenance fogged over, and emotion ceased to be visible on her face. She sighed, she shrugged, and, raising her clipboard, she passed on. I took my seat again, and have not stirred from my desk since then, hoping not to see anyone else or to be seen, despising everyone and everything around me and feeling that I in my turn am despised. I do not wish to join my colleagues or to flout them—I do not wish to do anything in this building, and so a kind of paralysis has come over me. The way I am sitting here hunched and immobile, my elbows drawn into my sides, I really must look like an invalid as Caroline had thought.

Imagine that this morning I had been light-hearted!

Wedged between the nightmares of last night and the oncoming awfulness of being at work today was an absurdly happy train ride in, a half an hour of peace which had no place in such a time of trouble as this. I read my Pascal and basked in the relief of my home not turning into a refugee camp, for this day at least. Dora had said she felt easier in her mind with my offer of help, and that was exactly how I felt in not having to give it. I had avoided an impossible fix, and Dora had found safety, and for the duration of the train journey even Fitch did not have possess me. I read my Pascal—he was trying to puzzle out the meaning of an odd Jesuitical term called *pouvoir prochain*, an article of faith which the learned members of the Sorbonne had decreed to be an essential tenet of the Church, in fact it was a heresy to deny it. What, then, did *pouvoir prochain* mean? Pascal wished to know, but every doctor of theology at the Sorbonne that he turned to for an explanation contradicted some other doctor, and one even claimed that they were duty-bound not to explain the term. Such inconsistency, however, did not trouble these erudite men in the slightest: it was the term itself, independent of any meaning assigned to it, that was sacred; and the sole requirement of being Catholic, according to the collective voice of that venerable, powerful institution in Paris, was to acknowledge that all the just possessed *pouvoir prochain*, whatever it was—thus making Pascal himself an apostate, he who could not affirm a thing he could not understand. Really, the Sorbonne was like one of those puppet parliaments whose members are always unanimous in their allegiance to the dictator. All those intelligent, ambitious clerics who had reached the pinnacle of their profession and must have been convinced of their authority to decide the all-important questions, these masters of their subject, were mere slaves to the majority opinion in this privileged body of men, all their reasoning and their *ex cathedra* judgments serving only one purpose: to strengthen their standing in the Sorbonne. One would not risk the mere suggestion of a possibility that one's standing might be shaken, not even if it meant casting others out into the darkness of damnation. Pascal laid bare the pure self-interest of these ostensibly upright men, which for thirty minutes comforted me to no end.

It appears that I am again to be interrupted in my doodling—or should I call it my marginalia, in the event that I have to answer for it? In advance of Priestley comes his commanding voice, growing toward me, not seeming to pause for breath but visibly holding someone captive, a subordinate by the sound of it. One doesn't welcome a voice like that—you'd listen in vain for any trace of lilt in it, or any pleasing inflection. Instead it's mostly functional, a large, solid vehicle for broadcasting analysis and synthesis, explanation, ratiocination—for public speech, not private. What can he want with me? I have this morning finished my task of rearranging the files into chronological order—but perhaps he and Fitch have, on second thought, decided that alphabetical order is after all the superior one, the system of classification nonpareil, and he is coming to inform me that I can get started right away on undoing the work I did, that is, if I am sure I recall all twenty-six letters in their proper sequence. Will I have to sing my ABCs for Priestley? This is the man I had once envisaged as a friend, whom I had called just a day after Jack's birth when we were still in the first flush of our joy and I was eager to share with him our glad tidings. My feelings for him had once been that warm.

So it's Larry Nolan he's been haranguing—the two of them fill up the entrance to my cubicle, looming presences, and when I look their way I'm still hunched at my desk as if I'm cringing from them. Priestley is not here to pass the time of day with me.

-Clark, we need you in Caroline's office.

-What for?

-She's doing an inspection and the phone has to be manned in case the Embassy calls.

-If Joe needs my help he can ask me for it.

-What?

-I don't take orders from you, Andrew.

-Who said you did? No one's giving orders, Clark. Someone's got to sit at Caroline's desk and you seem to be more available than anyone else right now.

-Then Joe can ask me himself.

-What difference does it make?

-To me it makes a difference.

-Jesus Christ, what a time to start carrying on. Alright, I'll tell you what—why don't you just keep on drawing your cartoons there and we'll get someone else to do it.

-That sounds like a good idea.

He regarded me for a moment as if I were some curious but morally objectionable creature, like the bearded lady in a freak show, and when he'd seen enough of the exhibit he moved on, with Larry Nolan trailing behind him, their retreat at least unaccompanied by that stentorian voice they'd approached with. I wish I could claim that I had given him a smooth rebuff, sending him on his thwarted way while I leaned back triumphant, but I had blushed and stuttered in my cramped position, and instead of staring him down I had just stared down, imagining how ridiculous I must seem to defy him over such an unimportant matter. I was shaken with anger, and as they walked off I asked myself in bewilderment, "How could I have done such an idiotic thing?"—by which I meant having invited him to my home right after Jack's birth, having singled him out to invite!—and suddenly I was justifying it to myself all over again: at the time I thought his two young girls would enjoy seeing a newborn, and also his wife and Ellen were on friendly terms. Indeed, I still remember how those girls cooed over Jack; they were quite delightful children themselves, thrilled at being asked to help give the baby a sponge bath and dress him.

Will I now have the pleasure of Fitch's company to look forward to? So many guests are calling that I think it must be my receiving day—I could use a manservant to bring me visiting cards on a silver salver. At least while I wait I have my margin drawing to occupy me, thanks to Priestley's kind words of encouragement—I do find that making silly sketches is more tolerable in one's despair than pretending to read government documents. There is also the spectacle out my window to keep me from having to fix a blank look on the indecipherable text in front of me: in the city square another ugly rally is taking place, and, more so than any of the others that I've seen, this one is unsettling. The crowd today is far greater in force than it was just two days ago, men by the hundreds crammed onto the plaza, and women too this time, a dense, combustible mass getting whipped up into a ferocious frenzy by some rabble-rouser on the platform—their roaring is savage and raw. What occasion could have flushed so many of these creatures out into broad daylight? And then rising above the swarm off in a corner, I am certain I can make out a trail of smoke, an odd feature on the landscape. They surely haven't started a bonfire to keep themselves warm, not with such a huge lot of them jammed together. Could they be burning someone in effigy—an American, a Jew?—or burning books? Either way it would be an ill omen, a very public turn for the worse. Something must have happened since Tuesday's rally to incite this mob, but what that is I do not know, since there has been no change in official policy this week, nothing the consulate or Embassy is aware of. There is a kind of aggrieved rage in their shouting, as if some wrong had been inflicted on them—although who could do it, and how? Lord, I even see children down there—a boy who can't be more than ten is drifting through the crowd alone; a small girl in pink earmuffs is clinging piggyback to her father. She looks about Jack's size, an innocent breathing in the badness around her, unaware—O it sickens me to imagine Jack down there, a fragile boy who doesn't yet suspect perversity in anyone. Such discoveries he has to make about the world; so many winds will blow his way, so many of them noxious, and some of them so insidious, even the cool evening breezes carrying disease. Will he be able to distinguish the fresh air from the pestilent?

I'm done with this office for the day. Fitch has had his chance to pay me a visit, and I cannot bear any longer to remain here, reduced as I am to hating the industry inside the consulate and witnessing the hatred outside of it. Everyone seems to be attaining their ends quite successfully without me, and since it is only I who am lacking a goal, it is time, I think, to make my purpose disappearing from this place until tomorrow morning, when at last this terrible week will somehow come to its conclusion.

FRIDAY

At breakfast

-Yes, I do believe that you feel sick, Jack. Do you believe me?

-Yes.

-And if your tummy really hurts you in school then they can call me and I'll come get you, alright?

-But my tummy hurts right now! I don't want to go to school.

-Not even to see your friends and play on the playground and have reading circle, which you love?

-No.

-Not even if I tell you a long bedtime story tonight? Or two stories—and one with a dragon in it? Alright, two dragons and one kindergarten boy. Not even then? You know, your tummy's only one part of you that feels bad, but I'll bet if you started counting all the things on your body which don't feel bad there would be at least a hundred. Like your elbows—do they hurt?

-No.

-Then what you should do is think about how good your elbows feel.

-But they don't feel good.

-You mean they feel bad?

-No, they don't feel anything.

-Well, you're lucky. How would you like to have a tummyache in your elbows, too?

-Elbows don't get tummyaches!

-Yours don't, but that's because they're healthy

elbows.

-But my tummy still hurts.

-I know it does, Jack. Listen, honey—every once in awhile Daddy absotively, posilutely has to be at work, and I'm afraid this is one of those days.

-What do you have to do at work?

-Today an important man is coming for a visit, and all of us, including me, need to be there.

-What's he going to do?

-We're not sure exactly. Maybe he wants to look around our building or talk to some of us. Maybe he has an announcement. Do you know what one of those is? When people tell you big things, like, "The king has chosen a new knight for his round table"— things like that. So I'm going to ask you to go to school today, and I'll write you a note to say that you woke up this morning with a tummyache—and while you're in school you can tell all your friends that tomorrow you'll be very very busy going to the airport to pick up your mommy.

-Daddy, what if we get to the airport and we can't find Mommy's plane?

-Oh, we'll find it. A plane can't hide that easily, you know.

-I wish we could be the first people at the airport tomorrow. Then Mommy could see us before anybody else.

-When Mommy gets off that plane she won't see anything but her very own Jack sitting high up on his Daddy's shoulders waving at her. How's your waving these days?

-When I wave my tummy hurts.

-So we'll save the waving for tomorrow.

I cannot even think about staying home today. By nine o'clock I have to be sitting at my desk working, or pretending to work, and if then Jack's school should call, after my presence has been noted, no one could accuse me of malingering. But to take a sick day on this day—come Monday I would be without a job. Jack truly is in some discomfort, though, and so something must be decided: not whether he's well enough to go to school—he probably isn't—but how to get him there, since one can hardly hand over to a teacher a squirming, moaning child. If I can keep diverting him with banter, the pain might go away—it's happened before with these stomachaches, my child becoming too intent on talking to remember his complaints. And if that fails then whatever it takes to convey Jack to his classroom will just have to do. This morning he will have poor parental care from me.

Actually, it would do us both some good to crawl back into bed. My body is yearning for the rest it didn't get in the night, when I was awakened again and again by strange noises outside, distant screaming it sounded like, and car horns blaring, and even glass breaking—or was that merely a dream? Some of last night's cacophony must have been a product of my sleep—for example, the crash of a television thrown from on high down to the pavement below, as I saw nothing unusual when I looked out the window this morning. But other disturbing sounds were real enough, and they reminded me of the raucous celebrations in Kovo whenever the football team wins a big match, drunken men taking to the streets in large numbers to triumph. I rather doubt, though, that this city had much to rejoice about throughout a frozen January night.

Could the ruckus I heard have been a spillover from that massive gathering yesterday in the city square? It was showing no signs of abating when I left work; indeed, it's impossible to imagine that such a riot could have ended peaceably, the crowd just dispersing as everyone went home for dinner. I suppose those nighttime noises were the remnants of the day's rage.

One does hope this latest disruption hasn't interfered with the ambassador's plans—it would put me completely out of sorts if the visit were postponed and all its attendant anxieties carried over into another week. The only comfort I've gotten out of this whole affair has been to see it confined within five days—but surely I'd know by now if something had changed, as Caroline at least would have called. I imagine that certain of my colleagues are in quite a state this morning as they prepare themselves to meet the ambassador, the moment almost here which seems to be less a part of time than the very culmination of it, after which whatever is, is not to be considered. Only today has any relevance, and so to talk of what is not of today would be to digress, which rather puts the clamp on me since all I could possibly have to say would be irrelevant. At these grandiose events which inspire the sort of awe-filled attention one might expect at a sighting of the Virgin Mother, I get a yen to talk of anything else, however trivial: an exchange of views on the local climate would do, or movies, sports—anything at all to keep myself uninvolved. There should be a god of proper perspectives to invoke when these occasions get too impressive, someone like the cynic Diogenes, who, being visited one day by no less a personage than Alexander of Macedonia and offered by him the granting of any favor, requested only that the great man stand aside so as not to block the sunlight.

It's quite likely that Dora in her hiding spot heard the same violent sounds last night that reached me. Those families must have felt completely exposed in such a conspicuous place as the synagogue, all too close to the center of town, where the hurly-burly which for me was only a distant disturbance would have filled their ears in another night of sleeplessness. And if that pane of glass I heard being shattered was not just a dream of mine then maybe they even had to listen, petrified, to their own windows getting smashed. Was the synagogue vandalized again, this time with Jews inside it? But if they were no longer secure in there, then surely one of them could have gotten to a telephone—Dora wouldn't have jeopardized her son's safety, however reluctant she was to impose on me. There must be at least one phone inside that building, and she had promised to call in the event of trouble—and I trust her as if she were an old dear friend, something to which a few days' worth of knowing her has not given me any right, but I can't help it, she has become in half a week like an intimate to me. Am I deceiving myself? I'm not one to form fast friendships; anyway, not like I once was, when the early hopeful signs in a person were enough to win my devotion, as they were, say, with Priestley. I've learned not to lose my head over those early signs, so why do I have such instinctive faith in this truly foreign woman that I only met on Tuesday?

Of course I may be mistaken about her. She hardly seems one to yield up the mysteries of her character so quickly. I feel sure, though, that she has treated me as an equal this week, not impudently but naturally, and thanks to her example I have treated her the same, however little the circumstances have warranted it. She didn't have to act so well toward me, either, not when she might just have been deferential. Or she could have tried to turn our contact to her advantage, and who would have blamed her if she had? Instead she has barely seemed to acknowledge that I have an official role, looking straight through the mist of rank and station to address me, and she is the only person in the consulate upstairs or down to have done so. Maybe that's why she initially refused my help: it would have gotten us off on the wrong footing. Is this equality I sense exclusive to her and me alone, our personalities precisely calibrated to be receptive to each other, or do we both just happen to share a disregard for differences in status? Well, it's really no matter now—time knows how to clear up the uncertainties of human connections, as it did with Fitch and me, all my inklings confirmed at a blow. Far more important at the moment than how she stands in relation to me is whether she would keep her word to me, and I do not doubt that she would.

*

The consulate

Something has happened in Kovo. Overnight an event has disturbed the peace on such a scale that it is already known across the city, for there's hardly a person I've seen this morning who hasn't registered the effects of some upsetting news—Jack's kindergarten teacher looked completely preoccupied when I dropped him off at school, seeming scarcely to hear a word I said about his stomach complaints, and on the train no one was reading the books and newspapers they carried, but passengers were questioning strangers next to them in low voices. And here at work the mood is anything but an expectant one; if the ambassador were to arrive right now he would take the staff by surprise. Only I in my ignorance followed instructions by coming in and getting straight down to work, while my colleagues have quite neglected Fitch's memo, instead forming themselves into their customary grouplets to confer about the rumors they've heard. Something apparently occurred at that huge rally yesterday, or after it, and Fitch is on the phone in his office trying to get information. I should have asked a stranger on the train myself.

The consulate is perfectly immaculate. The walls are bright, the floors gleam; in vases throughout the lobby stand tulips and lilies in perfect bloom, flowers impossible to find at this time of year and obtained, one assumes, from the same mysterious source as the fruit we feasted on. The place even smells just right, the strong odors of paint and ammonia and scouring powder having faded, except for vestiges of them which lag behind, suggesting cleanliness. The building waits exquisitely adorned to receive her visitor, poised for this one day or maybe just the morning in all her fresh anticipation.

Priestley, it's becoming clear to me, possesses a kind of genius. Not until now have I appreciated how supple a mind he has, not in political science, or interior decoration—in those areas he merely displays a facility, or call it a talent—but he is unsurpassed in the art of looking indispensable. I am sure it requires prodigious creative powers to appear forever occupied with a necessary agenda, especially in a moment of distraction like the one we are in. When no one knows whether the ambassador will even be here today, and the uncertainty of the situation has drained all sense of direction from everyone else, when every last detail in getting ready has been attended to, here is Priestley conjuring up still more details, magically producing determination even when there is nothing left to be determined about. It seems that he and Fitch spent a considerable stretch of time this week composing a mission statement for the consulate—lest there be any doubt about our zeal—and then mounted it in a glass case in the lobby for the perusal of the ambassador, should he happen to take a turn about the room—but Priestley has conceived the notion that the A. might fail to notice the glass case, which would nullify in a trice a week's intellectual exertions, and so he has requisitioned Caroline to help him tack up copies of the mission statement at various discernible spots along the way of the proposed tour. As he stopped near my cubicle to survey a cork bulletin board, sizing up the space as if he had a Rembrandt to hang there, I did wonder whether it really is his enterprises, large and small, which give birth to his purposeful manner, and not the manner itself breeding the enterprises.

But something has happened. What is it? I keep looking toward the closed door of Fitch's office where he's been holed up for almost an hour—a very odd sign, considering that our visitor was scheduled to arrive about now. Is he in there nerving himself to deliver some bad news to us, the ambassador kept away from Kovo because of the rioters, or worse, having made it to Kovo, had a run-in with them? Bad news, indeed; I would not like to be the one to announce that the consulate will after all go uninspected.

Apprehension is beginning to stir in me. All morning I have been puzzled by the strangeness around me, but now, in addition, I can sense the awakening of dread—of what I don't know. The absence of the ambassador is perplexing, but what do I care of him? Maybe it's Dora I'm fearful for, isolated as she is, or even Jack, who could be less than perfectly safe if hooligans are on the loose. If Ellen were in my place, I imagine she would just go fetch him from school and bring him home, her maternal instincts making him the priority at such a time as this. But whatever happened in the night, the city seems to be functioning in an orderly fashion today—school is in session, the trains were filled as usual. Nothing is keeping the citizens of Kovo from going to their daily destinations.

I feel that closed door as one feels the exercise of power over one, a reckless, willful sort of control that is exerted through non-exertion, Fitch merely staying closeted in his office while the rest of us wait fretfully for news. He must be aware that he has a hold on us in our state of suspense, his hold becoming firmer the longer his door separates him from us—and if this is not an assertion of his power, then what is to keep him from coming out and talking to us, whether or not he knows anything? Someone should go knock on his door to ask for information and end this anxious dependence on him—that someone, I suspect, being me.

-Clark, do you mind if I use your trash can to throw this paper away?

-Not at all, Caroline.

-I took everything off the bulletin board so I could put the mission statement up. Does it look straight to you?

-It looks fine.

-Andrew thinks the font size is too small, but it's not hard for me to read.

-Do you know anything more, Caroline?

-You mean about the ambassador? Well, we haven't heard that he isn't coming. I think he'll be here—it's only a few minutes past eleven now.

-But how about outside? There's been some incident in Kovo—hasn't there?

-That's what it seems like. Stan said there was a fire last night in a bookstore near his home, but no one else saw anything. There have been rumors, though.

-What kind of rumors?

-Well Betty and Larry were both told by different neighbors of theirs why they had that big demonstration yesterday—it was because on Wednesday two of those nationalists got killed. The story is that they started harassing a couple of Jewish men on a train, and the Jews were armed and fought back.

-My God. Are you sure the men were Jews?

-Betty heard that two skinheads had come up and demanded to see their passports, and the men had refused to show them. I guess that's when the trouble began.

-And what happened to them? Did they get away?

-We don't know. But Stan thinks if the story is true, then the nationalists are taking their revenge, and that the bookstore he saw probably had a Jewish owner.

-Maybe. It's hard to believe there's still a Jewish shopkeeper left in Kovo.

-Well, that's what Stan says.

-What other rumors have you heard?

-Nothing else. I'm sorry, Clark, I have to finish putting these up. Andrew's coming around to check them.

-Sure.

Fitch has emerged. My heart pounded just to look up and see the door perpendicular to the wall, the right angle indicating that news was here at last. Several of the staff hurried over to Fitch as soon as he came out, but instead of enlightening anyone he has summoned us all to the conference room, his expression betraying nothing of what he knows. Not even Priestley got a passing glance. What has he learned in the last hour to make this most jittery of men inscrutable?

-I don't want to keep repeating myself, so I'm going to talk to all of you at once. Caroline, don't bother taking minutes now—we won't be in here for long. This has been one hell of a frustrating morning, believe me. The phone lines around the city must be jammed with calls, because it took me forever to get any of mine through. So this is what I finally found out: the ambassador's plane has just landed in Kovo, and he'll be here in about half an hour. There's been a disturbance in the city as you probably know, and apparently because of that, they closed the airport last night and they've only just reopened it. I spoke to the ambassador himself a few minutes ago—he's fine, and said he was concerned about all of us. He wondered if we should be evacuated, but I assured him things weren't that bad.

-So what actually happened last night?

-Well, according to the French consul, that demonstration yesterday got out of control, and a bunch of hoodlums went a bit berserk—but the French think the target was property and not people. There's been some arson, some damage done to store-fronts, possibly some looting, but no one's heard gun-fire or seen anybody being assaulted.

-And who was this vandalism directed against?

-We know it wasn't against us or the French or apparently any other foreigners in the city.

-Then it must have been against the Jews. Does anyone know where those families from downstairs ended up going?

-Look, let's not rush to any conclusions. This incident happened just a matter of hours ago, and it's going to take a day or two to piece the thing together. We've had some civil unrest in Kovo and now it's over and the streets are quiet, and I'd like us to focus if we can on the visit. We're too well-prepared today to let that hurly-burly out there divert us. Now I see no rea-son why we can't stick to the original plan; if Andrew and I greet the ambassador and take him around the premises, and if the rest of you just treat this like a regular working day, there's a chance that we can

126

restore some order. I managed to reach the caterers and confirm that they're still coming, so unless you hear otherwise we'll all meet at 12:30 in the lunch-room. You've worked hard this week and you should be proud of yourselves. I don't think we could have done a better job.

Maybe I have misunderstood Vermeer. The comforting tranquility of those domestic scenes—the hush that settles over them—may go no deeper than the canvas; and rather than seeing only calm concentration in these women who are absorbed in their chores and handiwork, we are meant to infer in them an underlying unease, a hidden disquiet which suggests itself by the very means of their placid appearance. Perhaps even these simple female figures are subject to a paradox. I am aware of such a paradox in myself as I sit here filling out a form, the picture of quiet industry, while inwardly I have lost all composure.

Vermeer might have made fine use of Dora as a model for a painting. He could have caught her in that very moment when I first noticed her, an unrevealing woman attentive to the hanging up of laundry.

I am caught in this moment. Now for me is wholly this consulate this morning. Now is Fitch. I think other thoughts, but they have not released me from these circumstances—not even philosophical reflection has, not even prayer. Whatever self I have is hopelessly tangled in the particulars of this place and time.

I sense that something is required of me, now, here—but what? There is nothing to do except work, and wait. Indeed, we've been told not to do anything more than that, and I have no pressing business to take care of. What demand on me could this moment possibly have?

Fitch has retired to his office again, shutting the door behind him. It is a surprising gesture: with the ambassador due to arrive at any time, one would expect him to be darting about making a last-minute fuss, fiddling and meddling and peering nervously through the sparkling lobby windows. That is his manner, not this reclusiveness. If he's made his phone calls and given up all his news to us, and what he knows no longer separates us, why, then, does he still remain apart like that?

Perhaps he knows more than he is letting on. He might well try to keep from us any alarming news—a political assassination, say, or anything which could seriously alter the mood around here. He might try to keep himself from us if he is alarmed.

He didn't answer Betty when she asked about the families downstairs—but he couldn't possibly be aware of their hiding place, since no one could have told him. Still, her question was left hanging. She asked quite clearly about the families, and he did not say a word in response. Was there meaning in his lack of an answer, or did he just have more important things to consider than the whereabouts of those people?

No, the question would not simply float away if

one let go of it, diminishing in the mind's eye into nothing. It hovered, waiting for an answer, and it hovers now—but if Fitch had simply pleaded ignorance, or even lied to reassure us, that would have been enough to set the question free for a time. He owed us an answer, and he still does, and is this, then, what is required of me, to ask Fitch myself for the answer that was required of him? And does the moment demand it of me right here, right now?

Nobody but me seems to be in need of further information from him, and there is no urgency for me to find it out—surely it could wait until after the ambassador has left, when it would be easier to approach Fitch. I would be mad to knock on his door just minutes before the grand event commences.

He kicked those families out. He turned them out of doors because the ambassador's visit has for him an absolute value while everything else is relative. He sent them packing in the dead of winter, he won't even declare whether or not he has news of them, and I am willing to be patient. I am willing like Fitch to grant this visit precedence over every other consideration. The formal nature of this function makes any mention of Dora and her people inappropriate, and they shall be spoken of only when all the official speaking has been done, later if there's time and if not later, then another time.

No.
To delay even another minute would be unforgivable. The ambassador arriving before I have confronted Fitch would make final the utter abandonment

of those Jews. O let me not flinch from this folly.
Knock well: two firm raps: convey resolve.

-Who is it?

-Clark.

-It'll have to wait.

-It can't wait.

-Then come in. This had better be important
and it better be quick.

-You didn't answer Betty's question about the
families downstairs. I'd like to know if you have news
of them.

-Is this some kind of joke? You come to me
now with this? Get back to your desk, Clark.

-I'd like an answer first.

-Didn't you hear me? I just told you to leave.

-I'll leave when I have an answer.

-Christ, I was sure this would happen. I swore
to myself you'd find some way to inflict yourself on us
today—from the very start of his week I was wary of
you, because you march out of step and you think you
have the right to. You are the most self-absorbed person I have ever met. Now I am going to give you your
answer, and if then you don't get out of here you'll
regret it. Do I have news of those families? No. Have
I seen them or talked to them since they left, or talked
to anyone who does know about them? No.

-Then can you tell me if the vandalism last
night was against the Jews?

-You can draw your own conclusions there. It
wasn't against the Americans, so that pretty much nar-
rows the field, doesn't it?

-But do you know of any Jewish sites that were
vandalized?

-It depends on how you define a Jewish site,

and that I'm not doing right now because this conversation....

-The synagogue, for example.

-This conversation is over.

-Do you know if the synagogue was vandalized?

-I've already answered your question, and goddamit, if you don't get out of here now I'll call security.

-You do that, Joe, and when the ambassador comes I'll make a scene—I'll tell him you harbored refugees for weeks without his consent and then threw them to that pack of wolves out there—I'll disrupt this day in any way I can.

-Threw them to—? That's a lie. When they left here the streets of Kovo were perfectly calm. And we offered them escort which they refused.

-I'm asking you for simple information and nothing else. Was the synagogue vandalized?

-That is my understanding.

-How—broken glass—or worse? Was there fire? Was there a fire, Joe?

-According to the French there was.

-But there were people inside that building. Didn't they find anyone?

-They've found quite a few so far, but none that they've been able to identify. The French claim it's an ash heap and they're not even sure how many bodies there are, and until we do know more there's no point in speculating on who they were or what they were doing in there. If there aren't any dental records we may never find out. In any case it was a terrible event and that's why I've chosen not to upset the others by telling them now. Whether or not you can appreciate that....

-Joe, he's here! His car has just pulled up.

-Alright, Caroline, I'm coming. After he leaves, I intend to inform everybody about what I've just told you, which you can be certain is all that I know. Now if you'll excuse me....

*

The conference room

-We're honored to have Ambassador Todd with us today, and relieved of course that he's made it here safely. You must be feeling, sir, that Kovo is not a very welcoming place this morning, but I hope we can correct that impression during your visit here. When the ambassador arrived at the consulate a little while ago, he wanted to know right away how all of us were doing, and if anyone had been inconvenienced by the disturbances overnight, and he was eager to meet with everybody as soon as possible.

-Thank you, Joe. I'm relieved myself to be here—an hour ago I wasn't at all certain we'd even be able to land in Kovo, much less make it to the consulate. I can imagine that you are all very concerned about the violence in the city, and I want to assure you that you have the Embassy's full support, and that we consider your safety to be of paramount importance. I was glad to hear from Joe and Andrew that no one at the consulate was personally affected by last night's riots; but if they continue, we will offer you whatever help we can to keep you out of harm's way. Kovo may well be coming apart at the seams—in fact it's mainly on account of the instability in this region that I've come out here to speak to you today—and we're not willing to expose a single member of the Foreign Service to the dangers of civil unrest. Having said that, I also want to commend you for the fortitude you've shown throughout this troubling time. There is a lot of anti-American sentiment out there, some of it quite harsh, and plenty of lesser professionals than yourselves might have requested a transfer months ago, but not one of you has done so, which is a credit to you and to the country you serve. I do not doubt that the American consulate in Kovo has been a beacon of light in the middle of darkness.

-Now I must confess to a second reason for wishing to see you all right away: I'm afraid it's necessary for me to head back to the airport almost immediately. As you all know, the Economic Summit in Warsaw starts tomorrow, and I'm flying there directly from here—the preliminary talks begin today, and I've been asked to chair a meeting set for this afternoon. I regret that this means I won't be able to stay for lunch as I had originally hoped, especially since I've been eager to hear about some of your impressions of Kovo over recent months. They would be very interesting, I'm sure, and I'm sorry that there just isn't enough time today.

-The other thing there never seems to be enough of at the moment is money. The summit this weekend will consist largely of every country in Eastern Europe petitioning the U.S. to help rescue them from their various financial predicaments, but we won't be able to offer anyone much assistance, since these days we are having to pull in our own belts.

You are probably aware that the latest budget approved by Congress has sharply limited the amount of foreign aid available, and while they were busy on Capitol Hill withholding money overseas, they decided to reduce foreign spending in general. Not even the Foreign Service has escaped these cuts.

-I and my counterparts at American embassies around the world have been instructed to come up with some draconian cost-saving measures, which I had initially hoped we could do by means of something simple, like a hiring freeze. That proposal, however, proved quite inadequate in solving our problem. It would take me an hour to catalog all the schemes my staff and I devised to meet the new guidelines without affecting any of our personnel, but in the end it became clear that a larger sacrifice would have to be made. I have consulted with other ambassadors who are facing the same difficulties and even with the Secretary of State, and there seems to be no way out of taking the one step I had hoped to avoid, which is the closing of one of our consulates.

-You can imagine how excruciating a decision this was—I wouldn't wish it on anyone, I can tell you. After much debate, it was agreed upon that the chief criterion for keeping any consulate open would be the prospect of long-term economic and social stability in the region in question, and we eventually reached a consensus that the one city which clearly held out the least hope for prosperity of any sort was Kovo. The decline of the city is especially sad because of its great ancient history, and while I'm sure that someday it will recover from the state it's fallen into, we don't believe this will happen anytime soon—despite, I must add, your own efforts to foster development. You are all outstanding members of the diplomatic corps, and this decision to bring the Kovo operation to an end does not reflect in any way on the work you've done here, which has been exemplary, but only on an analysis of the city's growth potential—and I suppose the events of the last day have confirmed our view of things.

-I hardly need to say that this is the last kind of news I had wanted to bring you today, but I felt that you deserved to hear it from me in person. You will have many questions about the future, I'm sure—how much longer the consulate will remain open and whether you'll be reassigned, and if so, where, and these are details that have yet to be worked out. We would like to be able to place all of you in other foreign posts, but I must be frank in saying that our pockets no longer go as deep as they used to, and I fear there may have to be some reduction in force. At any rate, we should have a better picture within a couple of weeks, and we will then notify you.

-I think I'd better get back to the airport before it closes again. This has been a trying time for you, and the news I have brought you today will not make it less so. But I would like to leave you with one assurance at least: while the American flag flies in Kovo, you will be under its protection, and if the situation dictates that you should abandon the city earlier than planned, I personally will use what influence I have to ensure your safe and speedy departure from here.

*

Afternoon

How is it that those voices I strained to hear on the train this morning murmured below the threshold of my understanding while these ones behind me chatter above it, grating and glib and concealing nothing? Was it fear which hushed them earlier and which has now worn off? Or did those rush-hour commuters going to jobs possess a decorum which these midday passengers lack? Maybe it was an hour of the day before one is naturally voluble. Now the event is being discussed over noisily by two women a few seats back, and bits of their conversation reach me easily: the building was hundreds of years old; the blaze was visible for miles around; the trucks arrived in time to stop the fire from spreading but not in time to save the synagogue itself or anyone inside. These two old ladies might be sharing gossip, so unperturbedly do they seem to bandy about this news of the violent deaths of some people to whom they bear no relation, people in the abstract and therefore hardly people at all, but just symbols of people, representing the number of them dead, or the fact of their Jewishness.

Who will mourn any of them as particular persons? It is Dora they have killed—Dora and her child and her mother, and every other one of those helpless hunted souls. She is dead, and I perceived such life in her—that lovely liveliness which she kept close to her, as she kept her suffering close to her, reluctant to make a display of either. I caught a glimpse of the particular person that she was, and she won't be conjured up when they identify her by name or race or profession or any other detail attaching itself to her existence. That person has vanished forever, and either

God has taken her or she is no more, and I wonder what else there is besides my grief to mark her passing out of life. I don't even know who would recite the Kaddish for her, or for any of them. When word spreads of their destruction; prayers will be offered, but who will take it upon themselves to mourn them longer than a news cycle, to mourn them as a Jewish child should a parent? There is no one left to fulfill the obligation. Soon, then, they will be consigned to oblivion or fixed anonymously in an historical past, and beyond my sorrow, what is there to keep their memory alive, except, perhaps, the conscience of the murderers and their accomplices, and would one care to be consoled by that?

This could be the final irony, that those who most of all will never be able to rid themselves of the images of Dora and her child and her mother are the very ones who delivered them to their deaths—not the perpetrators themselves who must have assumed they were killing Jews instead of actual people, but those who made the killing possible, the facilitators who had seen the faces, and also those who failed to do enough —myself, for instance—who tried everything within reason to save the families, when what was called for was to abandon reason, to abandon myself and adopt any tactic, however desperate, that would have kept them all safe inside the consulate. I could have threatened Fitch, physically even, or begged his wife to intercede, called the Embassy to plead with the ambassador, called the *Times* or the *Herald Tribune*. I could have joined the refugees and insisted that Fitch expel me, too. While Dora and her child were being cast to barbarians I remained civilized; I comported myself within the norms of social conduct when those norms could do nothing to save innocent people from perishing in flames. How could a reasonable approach ever have succeeded with a man such as Fitch, who is no less terrible just because he too operates within the social norms, and justifies himself sensibly and is to all appearances ordinary? That terrible man could only have responded to threat or force or to a direct order, and I made no attempt to effect any of them. He had his awful way, and now we have seen the fruits of his decision, and one wishes him damned with those fruits so that they stick in his throat and choke and torment him, and never give him peace; but maybe instead he will convince himself that he was not to blame. Who knows if a sense of horror at what he has done will grow in him—or in Priestley, that clever man—or if, in the end, the occurrence will merely blend with others to form the impression of a memorably bad week, whose badness one experienced rather than participated in? If that is the case, if in his mind his deed does not stand starkly apart accusing him, but gets tangled in the whirl of the week's events, then I imagine he will suffer no consequence at all for his role in the murder of innocent people, since he will not be subjected to any proceeding to answer for his actions—he will not go to prison or lose his job or even be reprimanded. The ambassador himself made it clear to me that there would be no inquiry into this incident at the consulate, and more than that, he warned me not to pursue the matter, maintaining, however a genial demeanor throughout our brief exchange. When I found myself suddenly alone with him for a moment, free at last to speak my piece in the privacy of the men's room, the opportunity having finally come to make a direct appeal to him, only now it was too late; when I realized that it was just the two of us in there but I no longer had anything to persuade him of, a wave of nausea welled up in me— another one, for I had just hurried from the conference room to bend over the toilet, expecting to be sick. I had stayed in the stall for a minute or two, gagging and panting and dizzy, and when I emerged, lightheaded, I saw that the ambassador had come in and was standing at a urinal. He addressed me first; as I was raising handfuls of warm water to my face he joined me at the double-sink, and while he washed his hands, he said, "It really does make me sorry to see such a fine outfit as this break up. You can all be very proud of the work you've done here."

I was uncertain whether to respond to the large jowly man opposite me in the mirror or the one at my side, and so I stood awkwardly looking at his reflection, beads of water rolling down my face. "Thank you, Mr. Ambassador," I said. "It does come as something of a shock."

"It came as a shock to me, too, when they cut our budget like that." The image in the glass leaned toward mine, as if to confide in it. "It's all politics, you know—each party's out to prove it can spend less than the other, and it always seems to be in some area where no one has a constituency. Who's going to lose any votes if a consulate closes overseas?"

I nodded to confirm receipt of his statement. "There has been another shock, sir, that I feel you should know about."

"Oh yes?" He looked directly at me for the first time, and I had the impression that it was only then he realized that there was actually someone next to him, a subordinate with a name and a rank and a demand on his time, and the discovery did not seem to be a welcome one; he turned away from the mirror and pressed on the noisy hand-dryer so that I had to speak over it to be heard, and kneaded his thick hands under the hot air.

"A little while ago, Mr. Fitch told me that the synagogue in Kovo had been burned down in the night by rioters. Mr. Fitch said he learned this from the French consulate, which also told him that more than a dozen people had died in the fire. The victims were Jewish refugees we had given shelter to in our basement for several weeks. On Wednesday they were ordered to leave this consulate although, given the political situation in Kovo, Mr. Fitch can't have been unaware that such a decision would put their lives in danger. I know that they went to the synagogue from here because I was told so by one of the victims. They had nowhere else to go."

The dryer had gone quiet while I was talking, but the ambassador kept working his fleshy hands one into the other until I had finished, and then he extended one of them for me to shake. His grip seemed to enfold my own hand in his. "You must be Clark," he said, and of course I realized then that I had unburdened myself in vain. He looked at me with admiration. "It's a pleasure to meet you. When I arrived this morning, Joe mentioned that you especially were anxious about the minority groups in Kovo, and that you might want to raise the subject with me. And I'm glad you did. I think it's great that we have members of our Foreign Service like yourself who really care about the native population, and I know that Joe shares your concerns about the well-being not only of Americans in Kovo but also of the good citizens who wish to live

140

in peace. Clark, some pretty bad things have happened out there, and you and I both would like to have helped those in distress, but that just hasn't been feasible. It isn't our role here, and it would seriously jeopardize the safety of all the Americans in Kovo for any of us to get involved in the civil strife. It would also complicate relations between our two countries. I'm confident that you can understand the need for solidarity among the Americans. That's how you can help out, and it's also how you can help yourself." His expression was now that of a wise elder patiently explaining the world to a näive young man. "You're a good fellow, Clark, and I have a lot of faith in you," he said, patting me on the shoulder, and then he made his exit.

My encounter with the ambassador was so unexpected and ended so abruptly that it could have been a dream; I might have passed out in the men's room and only imagined myself in a small space with an imposing figure who crowded me out even at the mirror, who turned on a loud machine just when I began to speak and, worst of all, who would not show any signs of comprehending the message I was desperate to convey. It had the feel of a sleep-episode, but if I wasn't awake then, I'm not awake now, for there was no interval between my standing alone in the middle of that washroom and then walking out of that building to the train. It did happen; and yet the person I had talked with was indeed unreal. The powerful ambassador, this player on the world stage who commands such impressive attention, the prime mover of all our undertakings for the past week, is a phantom, insubstantial except in appearance. The man who possesses the grand title is a shadow of a man, attached to an illusion and quite willing to offer up his existence in exchange for it, and was it then for no one at all that such a week as this has taken place? Wherever he goes there is a stir, his presence charges the atmosphere, and many who meet the dignitary must long remember the occasion; but for all that he is unreal; while Dora, who may have vanished without a trace, and may even be forgotten and unmourned, Dora for whom there will be no eulogies or memorials, will have existence itself to remember her, and to remember what was done to her, and to her child and her mother, and to sort out the empty vessels from the filled, where we so miserably failed.

Jack will be surprised to see me when I pick him up from school. I didn't call ahead to say I was taking him out early, and my arrival will interrupt him in the middle of drawing a picture or listening to a story, Daddy standing incongruously there in the classroom. If I'm lucky I'll catch a few seconds of him being a schoolboy before he notices me and becomes my boy again. I will have my own story for him to listen to. How does one render such a tale gentle to a child's ears? "Do you remember the lady I told you about who gave you the little flute?" The question may be for a five-year-old, but what follows is not—and yet I must give him a child's portion of understanding. He should perceive, however dimly, that in addition to the ambassador's announcement, which will require us to find a new place to live, a new school, there has been a catastrophe. I'll present a version of the events when we are together again with Ellen and he has his mother's comfort close by—but this wholly vulnerable creature, my pure, unsuspecting child, must gradually be taught to see what people have it in them to do. That,

142

too, is education, the hardest learning of all, and I would have him slowly comprehend the misdirections of humankind, for there are many of them; and he will meet his share, in others and in himself. And if his family does not teach him to read the map of the heart, that maze of traps and dead ends, then who will guide him when he sets out by himself, and what will keep him from getting hopelessly lost, and how will he manage to find his way home?